Deadlier than the Male

Deadlier than the Male

LEIGH DANES

THE CHOIR PRESS

First published in the United Kingdom in 2025 by
The Choir Press

ISBN 978-1-78963-552-2

Prologue

If you are reading this, Ellen, then I must be dead. When you have read it, I hope you will remember the life we had with your father, and the fact that I love you above anything else in the world. You will find it difficult to believe that a loving wife and mother could have such a past. I hope you will be able to forgive and understand. In this envelope is the key to a safety deposit box in Switzerland, together with a letter of introduction. You will be surprised at the contents of that box, Ellen. You never knew that I was a rich woman before I met your father. I am not proud of the way in which I obtained that money, and I have never used any of it since I married your father. It is up to you what you do with it now. Give it all away if you want to, but use it wisely to help others.

Goodbye, Ellen, and may you find the happiness I found with you and your father.

Chapter 1

I had never intended to be a murderer, particularly not a serial murderer, but it turned out to be true that if you have killed once it is easy to kill again. If Charlie had not died, what followed might never have happened.

I first met Charlie when I was working as a waitress in a gentlemen's club in London. Not one of the upper-class clubs where women, even waitresses, were not allowed, but a perfectly respectable club for businessmen. Nor was it like the so-called gentlemen's clubs which abound nowadays.

I had to drop out of university as my father died and my mother was in ill health. I had a steady boyfriend at the time and, who knows, if I had finished my degree we might have got married, and my life would have followed the course laid out for most girls of the aspiring working class at the time. I would probably have been a teacher, got married, had children.

My tutor was very sympathetic and tried to get a bursary for me, but by that time the coffers were empty. I could have got a grant, but it wouldn't have been enough to keep me and my mother so, like many before me, I had to give up my formal education and find paying work. There was nothing much locally, so I went down to London hoping to make my fortune. Work was plentiful there; this was 1958 and things were beginning to look up, but there was nothing well paid for someone of my age with no experience and no qualifications – and living expenses were high.

Then my mother became even more ill, and I had to go home to nurse her. Three months later, she died, and I decided to go back to try my luck again in London.

I had been in full-time education for most of my life and had never seen anything of the real world. Needless to say, the real world was not interested in me, and I ended up in a comparatively low-paying job but in very pleasant surroundings, and the generous tips more than made up for my meagre pay. In fact, I could earn in a week more than I could have got in a month working in an office or a shop. Some of these tips had to be paid for by way of sexual innuendo and the odd hand on the bottom, but I found that I had a talent for dealing with this in a pleasant way without it going any further. I couldn't claim to be a beauty, but I was attractive and clearly gave out a hint of sexuality that men noticed. The climate was very different in those days.

Charlie wasn't one of the chancers. He was always extremely polite and friendly and always enquired how I was and what I was planning to do that evening. I was usually vague about this, not wanting to encourage him, but one day I told him I was going to a small arts cinema which was showing 1930s French films. He was clearly interested, and the next time I saw him he asked me what films I had seen. They were well known to him, and we happily discussed them. After that, we often discussed films and books and got to know each other quite well on what you might call a 'cultural' level.

One lunchtime, after I had served him, he called me back.

'I wonder if you would like these tickets to the opera, Lily. I was going with a friend, but he cried off and I don't fancy going on my own. It's a pity to waste them.'

I'd never been to an opera and fancied giving it a try, but as I had no friends who liked opera, I was going to refuse the tickets. Then the thought occurred to me that we could go together.

'I don't know anyone who would like opera.' I plucked up my courage and added, 'What about us going together?'

He accepted so quickly that I realised he'd had this in mind all the time.

It was then that I began to think more seriously about him. He was a good-looking man, what I think is now called a 'silver fox'. I knew that he was a widower with grown-up children. I also knew he must be wealthy. The question was, was he looking for a quick fling, a mistress, or had he something more permanent in mind? I decided to give it a go, and we had a very pleasant evening at a production of *Turandot*. I was entranced; I had never heard anything so exciting and beautiful. Charlie was delighted with my reaction and suggested we might do it again. He was perfectly polite, put me into a taxi and said he looked forward to seeing me at the club. So far so good.

I didn't see him for a few days as my shifts didn't coincide with his visits to the club, or perhaps he hadn't been in at all that week. He was a successful businessman, after all, and that doesn't happen by idling away your time. Then one Friday he came in just before I went off shift and asked whether I'd be interested in going to a concert the following night.

'I know it's short notice, but these tickets are like gold dust, and I've only just managed to get them.'

I did have a date but, weighing one thing against the other, I could see that Charlie was a better bet, so I accepted, and we arranged to meet in the bar at the Festival Hall. I enjoyed the concert, not as much as the opera, but Charlie seemed happy with my reaction.

'Are you hungry? What about a little supper?'

I hesitated but agreed, and we had a pleasant time finding out more about each other. At the end of the evening, he again put me into a taxi and sent me home. After that, we spent several evenings together over a period of weeks and got to know each other quite well. One evening, while we were drinking coffee after dinner, Charlie casually asked if I had ever been to Paris.

'No, but I'd love to. I've been to France; in fact, I spent the long vac in Normandy when I was doing A-levels and again while I was at university. I don't think I'll be able to afford to go again for some time, though,' I replied ruefully.

'You speak French then? How would you like to come with me? If your French is any good, you could be very helpful.' Seeing my hesitation, he quickly added, 'All above board, Lily, separate rooms. I have to go over next week for a couple of days and would enjoy showing you around. I know Paris pretty well but have no one to share its delights anymore. Not that it is the same as when I first went there before the war. I was in my twenties and found it all very romantic. In fact, I met my wife there.'

This was the first reference he had made to his wife, and I felt a wave of sympathy for him. Why shouldn't I go? It needn't lead to anything, and if it did, would that be so bad? It might just be the right time to find out his intentions.

'OK, let's do it, only I won't be able to go anywhere smart, I don't have the clothes. Let's just go to the odd but interesting sites and sights and eat in little bistros.'

He had the delicacy not to offer to buy me clothes and I respected him for that. I went home that night wondering if I was doing the right thing. I had decided that I wanted to become Charlie's wife, and going to Paris with him might give him the wrong idea altogether. I would just have to make sure that it didn't.

We went by car – with Charlie driving – and by ferry. There's nothing like that first arrival at a French port as it was in those days. You knew straight away that you were in a foreign country from the smells – garlic and Gauloises. It was so exciting.

Paris was wonderful. Having some idea by now how wealthy he was, I had feared that Charlie might have booked us into one of the expensive, flash hotels. I should have known better. In fact, we stayed in a charming nineteenth-century mansion in the Montmartre area. It had only five suites so was not crowded. It had a delightful garden where we breakfasted, watching the chickens peck about. It was that sort of place; comfortable but individual. It was the perfect location for exploring Montmartre. Charlie had known the area before the war, during the time when famous writers like Hemingway, F. Scott Fitzgerald and Gertrude Stein were there, and he said that it was totally changed.

'There are too many tourists of the sort who just want to see where the famous artists and writers hung out. They know nothing about their paintings or books. If you know where to look, you can still get a little of the feeling of that time, though.'

And Charlie knew where to look. We wandered round quaint little old lanes and, to my amazement, came upon a vineyard. It was very small and presumably didn't produce much wine. Charlie said that there were vineyards there in Roman times and that this one had been revived in 1928. We tasted some wine and sat in the sun, soaking up the atmosphere.

The next day, Charlie said that he would have to work in the morning and asked if I could accompany him to meetings and make sure that he understood anything that was said in French.

'I don't know if my French is up to it. I can read it, but I

5

really learnt to speak it while living with a French family and from my French friends.'

He looked at me quizzically. 'Boyfriends?' he asked.

'Yes, some,' I answered, blushing for some unaccountable reason.

'Close boyfriends?'

'It depends on what you call close. If you mean, did I sleep with them, then the answer is no. I was only eighteen, remember.'

Charlie smiled and looked pleased.

I attended some meetings with him during that afternoon and, to my surprise, I was able to be of help to him. Because there was a mixture of nationalities present, the meetings were conducted in English, but I translated for Charlie some of the private discussions I overheard between some of the French people present. This gave him the edge when it came to the final statements, and he was very pleased and very grateful.

Charlie was as good as his word. We had a delightful three days with no attempt on his part to take the relationship any further. He took me to the Père Lachaise cemetery. I found this rather an odd way of passing the time until he showed me some of the graves of famous people buried there. Interesting people like Oscar Wilde, La Fontaine (I didn't let on that I didn't know who he was at that time), Bizet, Proust (I had struggled with Proust for some time) and many more. We found the tomb of Héloïse and Abelard. I was very excited, but Charlie said it was just a way of attracting tourists. It had obviously worked because lovers and would-be lovers apparently came and put messages round the tomb.

When we returned home, Charlie, as usual, put me in a cab and said he looked forward to seeing me at the club.

The next time I saw him, he asked me out for dinner.

Nothing unusual in that, but he seemed nervous and very unlike his usual confident self.

I dressed very carefully, attractively but not too obviously. I was pretty sure he was going to ask me something important, but was it to be his wife or his mistress, or maybe even his secretary? He had been very impressed with my French.

During pre-dinner drinks he was very thoughtful and uncommunicative. I leant forward and put my hand on his. He started and I withdrew my hand quickly. It was the first physical contact we had ever had.

'Is something worrying you, Charlie? You seem very preoccupied.'

'Not worrying me exactly, but I must admit to being a little nervous. There is something I want to ask you, and I'm not sure whether to do it now when we both have clear heads, or to leave it until you have had some wine and might be more open to what I'm going to ask you.' He smiled to show that he was not serious.

'Although we haven't known each other for more than about six months, we get on pretty well, I think, Lily. I'm not getting any younger, and I feel that I have to grasp at any opportunity of happiness that comes my way. I am fully aware of the age gap, and I probably have no right to ask you but,' he paused, and I smiled encouragingly, 'would you do me the honour of becoming my wife?'

My heart started to pound, and the blood rushed to my face. 'Oh, Charlie,' I gasped. 'I'm the one who should feel honoured.'

I paused, looked down, then took the plunge.

'Charlie, from the way you reacted in Paris when we talked about my boyfriends, I feel I must tell you that I am not a virgin. After all, that was years ago, and I have been at university.'

Charlie smiled. 'If it comes to that, neither am I. Don't worry about that, Lily. I am not unrealistic. A lovely girl like you must have had lovers.'

'Not lovers, Charlie, just one.'

'Never mind about your lurid past, Lily. What is your answer?'

'Yes, oh yes.'

'I haven't bought you a ring, Lily, as I didn't want to appear presumptuous and, anyway, I was looking forward to the pleasure of taking you shopping.'

I felt a little dizzy. I couldn't believe this was actually happening. I had hoped that it would, and now I could look forward to a life of luxury. I will admit to being a little nervous about having to have sex with what was, to me, an old man, but that was the price I was prepared to pay. Was I a gold-digger? Perhaps, but I was genuinely fond of Charlie and admired him a great deal. I'm sure many marriages have been based on much less.

Chapter 2

The next couple of months were a magical whirl. Charlie had said that he wanted to take me shopping and he certainly followed through. First, we chose a ring, a beautiful ruby surrounded by diamonds, then we did some clothes shopping. He seemed to get as much pleasure out of it as I did. I suppose it was some time since he had had anyone to spoil and, although I didn't think it would last, it was very pleasant. Then one day, while we were having coffee, he said we ought to think about where we were going to live.

'I have a house in the country, which I'm sure you will love. When I'm in town, though, I usually stay in hotels or at one of my clubs. What about looking for a flat in London?'

I was thrilled, and we had a lovely time looking at the sort of flats that I could only imagine in the past. We found the perfect place in Mayfair. Looking back, I suppose it wasn't particularly special, but to me it was amazing. It had two bedrooms, each with its own dressing room and bathroom, a dining room, sitting room, a study and the most elegant kitchen with every possible gadget that was available at the time. I was delighted with it and couldn't wait to move in.

'Why don't you move in straight away, not wait until we are married?'

I made the move a week later, and that was the first night that we spent together. I was amazed at how enjoyable it was. I had been dreading it. However, Charlie turned out to be a wonderful lover, and the sex was much better than I'd ever known before. He was gentle and considerate, took his time and clearly knew what women liked. It was a revelation. I looked forward to a perfect marriage. Riches beyond anything I had ever known, a man I enjoyed being with, and a good sex life. What else could anyone ask for? We had an idyllic couple of weeks.

Then the idyll ended. Charlie said that I must meet his family. I was very nervous. It was inevitable that they would not be happy about his marrying again, especially to a much younger woman.

They were polite but clearly suspicious, and did not warm to me at all during the whole of the two hours or so that we spent together. You couldn't blame them. Charlie was much older than me and was not likely to outlive me. I knew that everyone in his family must have regarded me as a danger to their inheritance.

His eldest son, David, came to see me when it became clear that Charlie was serious and intended to marry me. If David had known me better, he might have taken a different tack. I was not unreasonable. I knew that Charlie had wide business interests and was extremely wealthy, although not as wealthy as he turned out to be. I did not expect that he would leave everything to me, but David assumed that that was what I was after. He came to see me in my new apartment, and you could see as he looked round that he had me pinned down in his mind.

He immediately took a firm line, refusing a drink and refusing even to sit down.

'You must know why I am here,' he began. 'You must see that what you are intending is impossible.'

'I understand that you must find it very difficult to accept, David, but I don't see why it is impossible. Charlie and I are happy together, and we would not be the first couple to have such an age gap.'

'You do not seem to realise the ramifications of my

10

father's business interests. If he were to change his will and leave everything to you, which he might very well do, particularly if you have a baby, the whole of our family's business empire could fall apart.'

I was surprised at his being so direct. I was also surprised at the thought that I might have a baby with Charlie. That had not occurred to me at all, and I was not sure how I felt about it.

'First of all, David, what makes you think he would change his will and leave everything to me? I'm sure Charlie wouldn't dream of doing such a thing, and I certainly wouldn't ask him to.'

'You say that now, but how do we know that you won't change your mind, or what influence you might bring to bear on him. Of course, I don't think that he would leave the businesses to you as such, but he might very well leave you such a huge amount of money that the whole enterprise might be undermined.'

'So this is all about money and the fact that you think I am a gold-digger?'

He looked shocked at my directness and didn't answer. Thinking quickly, I said, 'Have you heard of something called a pre-nuptial agreement? It's something they have in America.'

'Yes, of course I've heard of it, but what is that to do with this case?'

'Suppose that I agree to one in which Charlie leaves me a set amount and I will make no claim on anything else. Would that set your mind at rest?'

'Not really, no, it would not be binding in law.'

'No, I know that, but how would I look if I signed a pre-nuptial agreement then reneged on it and we ended up with a court case? I'd be spread all over the newspapers as a heartless gold-digger. I know we have to accept the fact that I will probably outlive Charlie, although you know there are no guarantees of these things, but I will be happy with the life that I will have with Charlie. It will be way beyond any dreams I might have had. I never thought I'd marry a rich man, particularly one as cultured as Charlie, and as kind as he is. We have so many things in common, and I'm sure I can make him happy. As to having a baby, that isn't a thing that I have ever thought about.'

David looked thoughtful. 'What sort of sum are you thinking of?'

'I don't know! I've never thought about it before. You clearly don't know me, David. I think you ought to try to understand my point of view. When I first got to know Charlie, I had no idea how rich he was. He was just a very pleasant man with whom I shared a lot of interests. It grew from there and I have no wish to either exploit him or try and cut the family out of his will. You have no right to assume that that's what I'm trying to do. Charlie wants the family to accept me and to get on with me. That is what I want too. I have experienced too much family discord to want to be involved in any more.'

'How do you mean, what family discord have you had?'

'It's too complicated to go into now. Suffice it to say that there were religious differences. My mother came from a Catholic family and married a Protestant. You can probably guess the rest.'

'Well, actually, I can't. Why did that make such a difference?'

'No, you probably don't know. I come from Liverpool originally, David, and the religious differences are still quite strong there. My mother's mother had died, and her father was ailing, so the oldest sister became what you might call matriarch of the family. She was very bigoted and would not recognise that my mother and father were really married. There was a lot of bitterness and in the end all contact was cut off. It was a problem for my mother all her life, and even towards the end, when I contacted her sister to let her know my mother was dying, she still didn't come to see her. So, you will see that it is important to me that there should be no estrangement between Charlie and his family.'

David sat thinking silently for a few moments and then seemed to come to a decision.

'I will speak to my father about this idea of yours then, and we will see what we can work out.'

I breathed a sigh of relief. I didn't want anything to endanger my marriage to Charlie.

'Is that the best way to go about it, do you think? Your father might see it as antagonism towards me. Maybe it would be better if I approached him first.'

'And what if he refuses to agree?'

'Well then, it will be time for you to step in. I will not say anything about our meeting today, and if he will not agree then I will suggest that he should speak to you about it. Between us, I am sure we can come up with something acceptable to everyone.'

David stood up and offered his hand. 'I am sorry if I've misjudged you, Lily, but I am sure you can see how it looked. A beautiful young woman like you and a man of my father's age.'

I took his hand; he held it for just a little longer than was necessary, and I knew that I had won this round.

Chapter 3

Charlie and I were married in a registry office, quietly, with just family present, and we had a delightful honeymoon tour of the Continent. Charlie laughingly called it our 'Grand Tour'.

The first rush of sexual desire didn't last, of course. After all, Charlie was sixty, but we still made love fairly often, and although it was always enjoyable, and I was always completely satisfied, it didn't happen often enough. I was very tempted to stray. I didn't, however, a fact of which I was rather more pleased than I should have been, as I had been brought up in a world where marital vows were taken seriously.

We had two happy years, during which I became used to a life I could have only dreamt of. Then disaster struck; Charlie had a heart attack and died. Although not heartbroken, I was very upset. I had liked Charlie and enjoyed his company. I was also scared of what the future would bring without his support and, let's face it, his money.

It was a huge funeral. I was surprised at the number of important people who attended. Charlie was more of a player than I had realised. I found it very wearing, as I had to greet so many strangers. Also, I was aware that members of the family resented my high profile.

Eventually, it was all over, and I was left alone in the flat wondering what I would do next. A lot would depend on what Charlie had left me in his will. I had signed a prenuptial agreement, of course, in which I would get the flat and £100,000 for each year of our marriage. So that meant I should have £200,000 clear, and that, as Denis Norden used to say, was a lot of money in those days. I could of course sell the flat, which was worth a good deal, but I decided to stay there for a while and do nothing precipitate. Everything depended on the will. For all I knew, the family had persuaded him to change it.

The reading of the will went smoothly, despite the tense atmosphere. I had been expecting some trouble from certain members of the family, but David had evidently talked everyone into agreeing and, although there was some muttering, no one raised an open objection. I think they were relieved that I hadn't asked for more.

David came to see me a few days later, bringing the family solicitor with him. They had a number of documents for me to sign and when this was over the solicitor left and I poured David a drink.

'What will you do now?'

'I don't know. It's only just sinking in that I have to make a life without Charlie. Don't look so cynical, David, you know what Charlie was like. Although he was kind and considerate, he automatically made all the decisions. Don't get me wrong; I liked being looked after and not having to take control of things so much myself. I'd had to do that for too long. The problem is, I have become used to being looked after. Now I am going to have to start making decisions for myself again.

'I think I will just quietly stay here for a while and give it some thought. I had thought that I might go back to university and finish my degree. I can afford to do that now, thanks to Charlie.' I laughed, but not very convincingly, and I could feel tears coming into my eyes, so I turned away to pour him another drink.

David came across and put his hand on my shoulder. I

had a sudden, possibly mistaken but quite strong, feeling that he was going to make a move on me. I had always known that he found me attractive, but surely he was not going to be so crass at this particular time. I looked at my watch and started.

'I'm sorry, David, I hadn't realised the time. I have an appointment with my bank manager.'

It broke the mood and David finished his drink, gave me a brief hug and left. I sat down, shaking slightly, not at all sure that I would have rejected him if he had made a pass at me. I hadn't had sex for some time, and they say bereavement brings all your strong emotions to the fore.

Chapter 4

The next year passed pleasantly enough. I stayed in the flat, with a few trips to Paris, Rome, Barcelona, etc. Just a few days in each, looking for fun and sex. I didn't bring anyone back to the flat or, indeed, let any of my 'passing ships' know where I lived. I had made contact with one or two people I had known at university, but their lives had moved on.

I started to assess my finances. £200,000 was a lot of money all right, but it was not going to last my lifetime. These days, of course, a young woman in my position might set up her own business, but that was unusual then and it did not even occur to me. I needed to find another rich husband, and I set about it methodically. They say that if you want to find a millionaire, then go where they go, so I started doing some research.

I thought that Claridge's would be a good hunting ground. Rich people, often men on their own, stayed there, so I decided to take a suite and see what I could find. But first I had to be suitably clothed. The things I wore for mooching about London museums and art galleries were fine for that, but they would not do for my new campaign. Nor would the sort of thing I wore on my sun, sangria and sex trips.

In the '60s, London became very fashionable, but it was difficult to find the sort of thing that I had in mind. I went down the King's Road, looking in the windows of the fashionable boutiques, but didn't see anything suitable. I knew I would have to go to Paris and find those discreet little boutiques with nothing in the window except for some tasteful pictures or perhaps a beautiful flower arrangement.

I decided that my best move would be to get in touch with the wife of one of Charlie's business associates in Paris. Amélie and I had got on rather well, and she was the epitome of what I was looking for. She was delighted to be consulted and took me first of all to her *corsetière*. I protested at this as I had a very good figure at that time and, anyway, people were throwing off all the old restrictions. She insisted, however, and said that no fashionable, smart French woman would dream of going out without being properly under-pinned. I pointed out that when the underpinnings came off, I would be revealed in all my falseness. She said that that didn't matter as my figure was good. What mattered was what the clothes looked like, and the right corset made the clothes look even better.

I bowed to her superior knowledge, and I have to say that she was right. Once I put on the underwear and the suits and the frocks that she helped me to find, I was amazed at the difference. I looked sensational. Smart, rich and sexy in a discreet ladylike way. I felt like a million dollars.

I was ready to start my campaign, so I booked a suite at Claridge's and moved in for the duration. I decided that my first move would be to take lunch and dinner in the restaur-ant, thereby establishing a presence. I felt pretty much at home sitting there. I knew that I looked good with my new Parisian clothes, and I enjoyed seeing the famous faces. I was particularly impressed on the day that Elizabeth Taylor and Richard Burton came in. It was interesting how discreet the other guests were. A murmur ran around the room, but no one looked directly at them. You cannot imagine that happening nowadays.

I became known to the staff but did not get any further in knowing other guests. One or two men of the lounge lizard type had tried to strike up an acquaintance, but I was not interested in them.

Amélie had given me some introductions, so I wrote to one of them and we arranged to meet for lunch in my suite, which clearly impressed her. I told her that my flat was being refurbished and that I was staying at the hotel until it was finished. We got on very well. She was very sympathetic, and I confided to her how much I missed Charlie.

'I have, how shall I put it, suffered bereavement before. Both of my parents are dead, but they were very ill for some time, and it was not unexpected. Charlie was such a lively, vibrant person that it came as a shock. He died so suddenly and after only two years. The past year has been very difficult and very lonely. I appreciated for the first time what "going into mourning" really meant. It is nothing to do with wearing black, but the suspension of your life.'

I stopped, as though too full of emotion to go on, and Margot leant forward and put her hand on mine.

'Don't worry, my dear, you will not be lonely any longer. I will make sure of that and, who knows, we might find someone to take Charlie's place.'

'That will be very difficult. I find young men so callow after Charlie, and I can't believe I will meet anyone like him again. Besides, I am not looking for a new relationship. I need time to be myself again.'

I smiled bravely and went on. 'I have taken the first step by changing my appearance. Amélie took me to the strangest little shops where they made me some beautiful clothes. She doesn't go to the big designers, you know.'

I laughed and she asked me what was amusing me.

'I am thinking of the first thing she made me do. She insisted on taking me to her *corsetière*. I was a little insulted at first, but she was right, as she was about everything. The

19

right "underpinnings", as she calls them, make all the difference to the lovely clothes she had made for me.'

By the time Margot left, she was eating out of my hand. I had struck just the right note of girlish frankness, and she couldn't wait to take me under her wing. Further meetings were arranged, which culminated in my being invited to a dinner party at her London home. I was sure that she had contacted Amélie to check up on me, but I didn't blame her, and I was sure that she would get a good report.

I checked out of Claridge's and went back to my flat. There was now no need to impress anyone, and I needed to husband my resources.

I was to learn that Margot never had more than ten round the table. She considered that number large enough for varied conversation but small enough for a level of intimacy, and I cannot say that she was wrong. From this, a number of invitations to other intimate dinners and cocktail parties followed.

I realised quite early on that two or three unattached men were always present. Margot had evidently enlisted the help of her various friends in finding me a new husband. I found it quite amusing, although none of the men came anywhere near Charlie's standard. That is until Jonathan Antrobus appeared on the scene. He had been out of the country for a while, which explained why I hadn't met him before. I found him very interesting, not least because he was a very handsome man. I am rather shallow in that way, and what a man looks like is very important to me. But he didn't just look good; he was an interesting man with varied intellectual pursuits.

He had not made his money but had inherited it, and was managing it well. This of course I did not find out straight away, but Margot found out as much as she could about all my prospective husbands and passed it all on to me. I protested of course, pointing out that I was not looking for a husband, but nonetheless stored all the information away for future use. Jonathan was present at the next cocktail party and made a point of talking to me. Before the evening ended, he asked for my telephone number, which I gave him. I had more or less decided that he was going to be the one. We did all the usual things; opera, concerts, theatre, cinema. Then one day he asked me if I'd ever been racing, horse racing, that is.

'No, I haven't, but I'd like to. What had you in mind?'

'I've been invited to what they call a "Friday to Monday", what you or I would call a weekend, at a friend's country house. It's near a course, and they are keen racegoers, so it could be fun.'

I accepted and three weeks later we motored down to what turned out to be more of a palace than a house. You might think that I would be overwhelmed, but in fact I revelled in it. It might have been worse if I hadn't visited a number of houses of the type, using my National Trust membership, of course. I had never thought that I would ever stay in such a place, though.

The entrance hall was huge, with a massive fireplace at one side. There was no fire, the weather being warm, but there was a beautiful flower arrangement in what looked like an antique Chinese vase. The walls were wood panelled and there was a magnificent staircase leading up to a galleried landing. What looked like valuable paintings were everywhere, some portraits and some landscapes. I learnt during the weekend that most of the portraits were of ancestors and family members, with a couple of visiting royals from the past. This really was high society.

The host and hostess were friendly enough, although I got

the impression that they thought I was just another of Jonathan's 'little friends'. The other guests were mainly as aristocratic as our hosts, although there were a couple of what used to be called 'the *demi-monde*' – showbusiness royalty.

I enjoyed my stay there. The food was good, the accommodation, while magnificent, was not quite as luxurious as I had become used to in my cosy Mayfair flat. These country houses were rarely warm enough in those days, and the plumbing was dreadful, but I could cope with that. The racing was exciting. I had a few bets and came away with a small profit. The money was not important, of course. It is the fun of watching your fancy go first past the winning post. Some of our company lost quite heavily but did not show any emotion, as that would not be seemly. Jonathan was sure that some of them could ill afford to lose, though.

'They are all class and no money, some of them,' he said, clearly amused. 'They need to find rich wives, and I know that at least two of them are planning to go to America to see what they can find – the opposite of what young American heiresses used to do in the 1800s.'

On the way back to London, Jonathan asked if I had enjoyed the experience, and I was able to reply truthfully that I had. He was quiet for a while then said, 'You know, one of the many things I like about you is that you know who you are and are happy with it.'

'How do you mean?'

'I knew another girl like you, that is, from what you might call "humble origins". He smiled to show that he was not serious. 'I thought she might be the one to replace my first wife, but when I took her to a country house, not the one we've just been to but with more or less the same company, she changed completely. She started to imitate the speech and mannerisms of the other women, trying to fit in with them.

'You didn't do that, you remained who you are, and I like that in you. So did the others. They are an untrustworthy lot in many respects, but the one thing they all have in common is that they also know who they are, because they have been aristocrats for generations. They all had a great respect for you because you are obviously happy in your own skin. More than one told me I need look no further – you know what people can be like with a single man, they can't rest until they have you married.'

'Why would you not look among your own class for a wife?'

'Because I haven't found one who is interested in the things that I like, or if I do meet what you might call "a suitable woman", she is already married.'

'Why do you need to marry at all? I would have thought you had a pretty good life as it is.'

'Yes, that is true, but I miss having someone close to me, someone I can discuss things with and who is on my side, as it were.'

'Are you proposing to me?' I asked, smiling to show I was not serious.

'I suppose I am, although this is not how I intended to do it. I had something more romantic in mind, not going down on one knee, of course, but in better surroundings.'

'I don't think that matters. I am not without sentiment, but I'm not sentimental.'

'So, what's your answer?'

I pretended to think for a while. 'Do you think we've known each other long enough? I know we get on well and I am pretty sure that I love you, but we are from very different backgrounds.'

'So were you and Charlie, and that seems to have worked well.'

'That's true, and at least I am financially independent, so no one would think I was marrying you for your money.'

'Is that a yes?'

'Do you know, I think it is!'

He pulled over to the side of the road and put his arms round me. 'You won't regret it, Lily. I'll do my best to make you happy.'

'Me too.'

He kissed me gently and we sat for a while in each other's arms. My pulse was racing. I'd done it. I'd pulled it off again. Life was once more going to be one of luxury and security. I wouldn't have been so happy if I had known what Jonathan could be like.

Chapter 5

At first, everything went well. Jonathan was delighted with what he called his 'lovely young wife', and I was happy to have such a handsome, rich husband. He was much younger than Charlie, in his early fifties, and I expected a much livelier sex life. It was fine at first but after a few months, when the first flush had died down, he began to find it more difficult to get an erection. I did what I could, and things improved, but one night, after I tried everything, stripping seductively, using my hands, tongue, breasts, anything I could think of, he tried again but without success and he grew angry and hit me. I was too shocked to say anything, and he hit me again. This excited him and he began to feel something. He continued hitting me until he had managed to come inside me and lay panting by my side.

I was in shock and, worse, I was having difficulty breathing. Jonathan realised something was wrong and began to pay some attention to me. He was obviously shocked by what he saw. My face must have already been reddening from the blows, and I was gasping with pain.

'Call an ambulance,' I said, choking. 'I think my lung is punctured.'

He leapt up and ran to the phone, and I heard him asking for an ambulance to come quickly.

He came back to the bedside.

'Bring me some clothes,' I gasped. 'I can't go to the hospital like this.'

He brought a nightdress and helped me to get it on just in time; the ambulance could be heard coming up the drive.

The medics were very efficient, and I was soon at the hospital being X-rayed. I had a broken rib, which had pierced a lung, and I was in hospital for several days.

'Don't worry,' the doctor said, 'we can inflate the lung, and it will soon heal itself. How did it happen?'

I looked at Jonathan, who looked pleadingly back.

'I tripped over my nightdress and fell down the stairs,' I replied.

I don't think the doctor believed me, but he wrote it down on the notes and that was that.

Jonathan begged for forgiveness and swore that it would never happen again. Margot, whom I allowed to wheedle it out of me, tried to persuade me to leave him.

'We all suspected that he wasn't very nice to his first wife, but we never suspected that he was violent.'

'Maybe he wasn't. He was much younger then and maybe didn't have trouble getting it up.'

'Maybe, but looking back I can remember her having bruises, which she explained away by saying that she had fallen from a horse. Which was very believable, of course.'

'Well, he says he is very sorry and wants me to give him another chance, and I think I ought to. He confessed that he had been drinking too much but swore that he would stop. If it happens again, though, I will bring charges, and I think he knows that.'

Margot wasn't convinced, and I knew that she was right. Violent men rarely change, and having realised that the problem was caused by his drinking, and knowing that he would never give it up, I had no faith in his promises but agreed to give him another chance. Everything was fine for a while, then it happened again.

That made me sure that I would have to take action, but what? I could sue for divorce, but it would be his word against mine. He would be able to produce the evidence of the first doctor I had seen, and there were no obvious signs on my body this time. I decided to kill him. It surprised me that I could be so cold-blooded about it. I had been finding out things about myself over the last couple of years, so this was just another facet of my personality which was being revealed to me. I wondered if it was because I had spent my early years in an orphanage and had not had anyone to bond with.

Anyway, I had decided to kill Jonathan. Oddly, it wasn't the physical pain he caused me that made me decide he deserved to die. It was the feeling of humiliation and powerlessness. I hated him, certainly, but I was also disappointed. I hadn't realised he was that sort of man. I had never come across men who would harm a woman.

I knew that Jonathan had a slight heart problem, so I began to think about how I could induce a heart attack. I read an article about a man who died after taking an aphrodisiac called Spanish Fly. What this was I had no idea, but it was worth trying. But how to get it? I bought a magazine from a shop in Soho which had advertisements for all sorts of odd things, and Spanish Fly was one of them. I disguised myself as a man, not difficult with the right clothes, a hat, false moustache and dark glasses. I then arranged a post restante with a shop in Soho and ordered by mail in Jonathan's name. People in such establishments don't look closely at their customers.

After that, it was easy. I followed the instructions, except that I doubled the dose, and a week or so later Jonathan had an attack. We were staying at my flat and I was out at the time. It was the maid's day off and Jonathan was alone. He collapsed, and it was several hours before I came home and found him. It couldn't have worked out better. If I had been home, I would have had to call an ambulance and his life might have been saved. As it was, I found him dead, and nothing could be done.

There was a post-mortem, of course, and the aphrodisiac found in his body. I was questioned by the police but denied any knowledge of it. The policeman was very sympathetic but was obviously puzzled. You could see that he was wondering why a man would need an aphrodisiac with an attractive young wife. With a great show of reluctance, I told him that things had been rather difficult in the bedroom for a while.

'When we were first married, my husband was very affectionate but, after a few months, there had been some ...' here, I paused in an embarrassed manner '... unfortunate incidents.'

I explained that this had bothered Jonathan a great deal but that I had reassured him, as women do, that it was not important. What mattered was that we enjoyed being together, that we were good friends, and that we liked doing the same things. I said that I had thought that Jonathan was reassured by this, but clearly this was not so. I told the policeman that I had suggested we should not try to make love for a while to see if this helped. Jonathan had agreed and for several weeks we had done nothing more than what you might call cuddle. However, he had suddenly rediscovered his ability, and I now realised this must be due to the aphrodisiac.

There was an inquest, of course, but I turned up in a discreet black outfit, with an enchanting little hat, and gave my evidence in a quiet but clear manner. My account was accepted as completely reasonable, and I was left an even richer widow than before, as I was left the whole estate.

Not unreasonably, his family, however, were not willing to

accept this. They challenged the will, claiming undue influence, and produced a pre-nup which stated that if the marriage ended, by whatever means, I would be entitled to a one-off payment of £100,000 for each year of the marriage. The family consulted a lawyer, who pointed out that pre-nups have no power in law and that the will stood. The family did not accept this and decided to go to law. They were all rich in their own right and could afford to go to law. I wasn't poor but didn't want to waste any of what I regarded as my hard-earned money. Also, any monies due to me would have been held up until the case was settled. I discussed with my lawyer what might be a reasonable division of the spoils. I was willing to accept the provisions of a previous will, in which I would get a third of the estate and the family most of the rest – barring some charitable donations. Why Jonathan had changed his will, I don't know. Maybe he felt guilty, or perhaps he didn't want his sons-in-law to get his money.

My lawyer put this to the family, and most of them were willing to accept it. However, his eldest daughter started saying that I was not entitled to anything as I had inveigled him into marriage and had probably killed him. I consulted my lawyer again and told him that in view of this, I was not sure that I could agree to setting aside the will in which I was the sole beneficiary. I allowed myself to be convinced that the best thing to do was to ignore the daughter, agree to a third of the estate and get the whole thing settled. I had intended do this all along but just wanted to put up a show of outrage.

I was exultant – I had got away with it, and it was time to pick up the threads of my life. What to do next? I went to my usual thinking place, the British Museum, and wandered round without really noticing where I was. It was in the

Egyptian section that I began to get the feeling that I was being followed. I ignored it at first. I always have a strange sensation in that section; the mummies give the place an eerie feeling for me. I moved on until I came to a large glass case containing various artefacts when I saw, or thought I saw, reflected in the glass, a figure I had noticed before. It was a man. Nothing strange about that except that he didn't look like the usual museum-goer. I mean, he didn't look like a tourist, or someone interested in history or different cultures. He hardly looked at anything, just wandered around trying to look nonchalant.

I went out and down the stairs to the entrance hall and hovered about looking at the notices. I was pretty sure that he had followed me, so I went outside and sat on the steps, pretending to study the guide I had in my hand. He came out and passed me, and I thought he was leaving and that I had been mistaken. He stopped at the bottom of the steps and lit a cigarette. He stood looking up and down the street, as though waiting for someone, so I went back in and headed for the Montague Place exit. I walked towards Russell Square, into the Russell Hotel and waited at the concierge's desk. The man must have followed me all the way, although I hadn't spotted him, because he walked quickly into the hotel, saw me looking and headed for the bar.

'May I be of service?'

I assumed a worried expression and leant towards the concierge.

'This may sound strange, but I think a man is following me. Would you be so kind as to ring for a car for me?'

He was all concern. 'Certainly, madam, you come with me, and I will arrange everything.'

He led me into his office and indicated that I should sit down while he talked on the telephone.

'The car will be here in five minutes, madam. If you wait here, I will come and escort you to it when it arrives.'

I thanked him sincerely and, true to his word, within hardly more than five minutes I was being driven away. For a short time, I was very pleased with myself, but then I started to wonder who he was and why would anyone be following me. Was it all my imagination? After all, it had happened only once, and there was no reason why a man shouldn't be in the British Museum and then go to a hotel for a drink.

Nothing else happened for a while and I had convinced myself that I was being silly, when I saw him again. I had gone to investigate Carnaby Street, which was very fashionable at the time. Frankly, I was disappointed as it seemed very tatty to me – and noisy. Every shop had pop music blaring out. I suppose if I had been a teenager instead of in my late twenties, I might have been more impressed. Anyway, I was walking past the shops and looking in the windows – 'Lord John' and 'I Was Lord Kitchener's Valet' are a couple I remember. I stopped and looked in the window of a shop on a corner called 'Irvine Sellars' when I thought I saw, reflected in the glass, the man who had appeared to be following me in Bloomsbury. I turned quickly and there he was, on the other side of the road. He walked off when he saw me looking, but it was definitely him. It had to be something to do with Jonathan's death. It had to be the daughter. She had not been happy about the settlement, although she had been persuaded to accept it. Had she decided to employ someone to follow me and try to find evidence for her suspicions? I decided to get my own investigator to find out what the daughter's man knew.

But how to do that? I remembered the very pleasant police inspector who had interviewed me during the investigation into Jonathan's death and went to see him and told him that I thought I was being followed.

'Maybe I'm being paranoid but, now that I am a very rich woman, I fear being kidnapped and would like to employ a bodyguard. Do you know of any reliable security companies who might be of use to me?'

'Well, Mrs Antrobus, officially, I cannot recommend anyone, but if you produce a list of security companies, I could tick the ones I thought were trustworthy.'

This opened another line of thought to me. If I could find an efficient but corruptible bodyguard, he could find out what the other man knew. He could bribe him or deal with him in some other way. I made out a list of names I had found from various sources and presented it to the kindly police officer. He handed it back to me with, I was pleased to see, very few ticks.

I interviewed some of the ones without ticks, most of whom struck me as incompetent rather than dishonest, but one did stand out. His name was James, Bob James, and he seemed quite bright, so I told him I thought I was being followed and feared kidnap and that I wanted him to shadow me for a few days and see if it was true.

'I can do that. Just keep me in touch with your activities and leave the rest to me.'

We agreed a price and I waited to see what would happen. It didn't take long. Bob rang me a couple of days later and we met in a bar in town.

'You're definitely being followed and, as it happens, I know the man. I've spoken to him, and he says that it is a Mrs Barber who has hired him. I assume you know her.'

'Yes, I do. She is my late husband's daughter. I think I told you that I was recently widowed. Well, Carol Barber does not think I am entitled to my husband's money. I assume she is trying to find some way of discrediting me. What she hopes to find out I cannot imagine, but at least I now know what is going on. Have you asked your friend what he has found out, if anything?'

'I gather that your husband died of a heart attack brought on by taking aphrodisiacs.' He looked enquiringly at me, and I nodded. 'Well, Mrs Barber is convinced that you gave them to him with a view to killing him.'

'That's ridiculous. Jonathan obtained them himself. I didn't even know he was taking them.'

'No doubt. However, my fellow detective reckons he is on to whoever bought the stuff in the first place.'

I decided to take a calculated risk and offered my man £50,000 to pay off the other man for whatever he would accept. He could keep the rest for himself. I told him that Jonathan's daughter had a bee in her bonnet and was trying to make sure that I didn't get my fair share of my husband's bequest. He took the money, assuring me that would be the last I would hear of the matter.

After waiting anxiously for a month, I got a call from my solicitor asking me to go to see him. I went with some trepidation and sat down opposite him.

'I'm pleased to tell you, Mrs Antrobus, that I have heard from the family's solicitor that the matter will be dropped. No explanation was given, but I suppose they have managed to convince Mrs Barber that nothing will come of spending more money trying to break the will. Whatever the reason, I think we can congratulate ourselves that we have heard the last of the matter.'

I thanked him and left in high spirits.

Chapter 6

The question now was what to do next? I got in touch with a couple of people I'd known at university, but they all had things to do. Vickie and Lisa had jobs, Pam was doing a postgrad course and Jenny was married and expecting a baby. They all had aims in life and I had none. I thought that being rich would bring its own rewards, and for a while it had, but when it came right down to it, I was bored.

Should I go back into education? I seriously considered it and even got some brochures, but the thought of being a student again at the age of twenty-seven and mixing with a lot of kids was not very enticing. I even considered charity work, but I couldn't really see me doing that. I didn't have the commitment for anything like that. Besides, I didn't really fancy mixing with the unfortunate. I didn't mind giving some of my wealth to a worthy cause, perhaps a charity that helped girls like me to go to university. The education was free, but there were many costs involved, as I knew only too well. I didn't give it too much thought, though.

It was while I was at the hairdresser's that I started the next part of my life. I was sitting next to a smart-looking woman who was talking to the hairdresser about a charity lunch she was organising. I suppose it was interesting to me because of the vague thoughts I had been having about doing some good. Maybe I thought that it might bring me brownie points to balance the fact that I had killed someone. I still had a vague belief in God at that time. When we were both under the dryer, I smiled and struck up a conversation.

'I hope you won't think me rude, but I couldn't help overhearing your conversation. Is the lunch open to anyone or just members? I'm new to the area and am looking to make some contacts.'

She appraised me, taking in my expensive clothes. 'It's open to anyone who is interested in helping the less fortunate, and who can pay the cost.' She laughed to show that she was not trying to put me off.

'That sounds like me,' I said lightly. 'How do I go about it?'

She explained that they were having a lunch and auction to raise money for an educational trust in Africa. That really got my interest, and before we parted, we had exchanged telephone numbers, and she promised to invite me to the next meeting. I was quite pleased. This could be the very thing I was looking for.

True to her word, she rang the next day and invited me to coffee at her house in Hampstead. It was a large house, in its own grounds. She was clearly not short of money. I found out later, when we were bosom pals, that her husband was 'something in the city', and whatever that 'something' was, he clearly made pots of money. Once again, I had found myself with the right people.

The lunch cost £25 a plate – a mere bagatelle to me now, and I happily signed up. Betty, that was her name, co-opted me onto the committee and I met more new friends. Not that I felt any particular affection for them! You may think that I'm cold, but I didn't notice any warmth in any of them. They were what later came to be called 'ladies who lunch'. Women with rich husbands and time on their hands. Charity wasn't their only pastime, of course. Many were having affairs, often with each other's husbands. I was introduced as Mrs Antrobus, and they assumed there was a husband in the background. I didn't disabuse them, as I didn't want to be seen as a danger – single women and widows are not welcome in these circles.

There was quite a lot of alcohol consumed at these so-called committee meetings. Not by me, I would pretend to keep up with them but managed to drink only one glass of whatever was going round. I had to keep my cool and watch my tongue. At last, the meetings were finished, and the day of the lunch arrived. By the time we got to the fourth course, with a different wine with each, I was becoming somewhat disillusioned with these philanthropic ladies. They were supposed to be raising money to help the disadvantaged, and they were stuffing themselves with expensive food like pigs. They would have been better giving the £25 directly to the charity. *Still*, I thought, *the auction will raise more, so it might all work out in the end.*

The auction started and I have never seen such a lack of enthusiasm. They didn't seem to get what it was about, and only bid for things they really wanted, leaving all the little, inexpensive things alone or only bidding low. I couldn't stand it so started pushing up the bidding on, first, a packet of cereal, and then on the other cheaper items. There was some craning of necks to see who was bidding up the rubbish, and some of the others, feeling shamed, I suppose, started to do the same. Most didn't, of course, so I decided to do my best to thwart them. The best item was left until last – a beautiful crystal vase. It was clearly worth hundreds, and there were those present who were hoping to get it for much less.

The bidding started at £20 and soon rose to £100, then began to tail off and only go up in £1 bids. I hadn't made a bid but when it got to £120, I bid it up by £10. This caused something of a stir, and someone went up to £140. I countered with £150. A murmur rustled round the room and Betty came over to me, looking nervous.

'Lily,' she whispered, 'it would be better if you dropped out now. Helen really wants that vase.'

'I thought the idea was to raise as much as possible for the Trust,' I whispered back.

'Yes, it is, of course, but Helen is a very powerful woman in the organisation, and she really wants that vase. It's a one-off, especially made for the occasion.'

'Then she will have to outbid me,' I said, smiling sweetly.

The auctioneer was looking at me, as was everyone else.

'Are you all done, madam?'

'What was the last bid?'

'£160, madam.'

'£200,' I said. 'We must raise as much as we can for the Trust.'

A brief smattering of applause ran round the room but soon stopped as Helen stood up, turned round and faced me. I thought I had the capacity for hate, but I wasn't in it with her. I am sure she would have happily killed me. I was more than a match for her, of course. I had in fact killed out of hate, while she could only dream of it.

'Come on, Helen,' I said, 'let's raise more for the Trust.'

She didn't respond, just stood looking at me then sat down again.

'Sold to the lady in the blue,' said the auctioneer cheerily, and the applause broke out again, this time much more widespread. Helen had met her match. To rub it in, I walked up to Helen and held out the vase.

'Here you are, Helen. If you want it so much, you had better have it.'

She took it automatically and another wave of applause rang out. It was sickening the way Helen's ex-sycophants gathered round me. I got away from them on the grounds that I had to settle with the auctioneer, paid up, walked out and never saw any of them again.

Chapter 7

I still felt restless. When I was at university, someone had the idea for a trip down the Spanish coast. It had never happened; no one had any money. I had plenty of money now, though. Could I do it alone? I could fly to Barcelona and hire a car there, then trickle down the coast. If I didn't enjoy it, I could always leave the car at an airport and fly home. I was getting used to the idea that I could do more or less anything I wanted.

A week later, I was driving out of Barcelona Airport and heading south. The weather in England had started to get wetter and colder, so it was lovely to drive within sight of the Mediterranean in the sunshine. I turned off and drove down to a little restaurant by the sea for lunch and had tortilla and calamares with lovely homemade bread. I hadn't felt so relaxed for some time. Who needed company? Not me!

I spent the night in a little pensione, where I tasted Rioja for the first time. The proprietor and his wife fussed round me, obviously worried about a young lady being alone. I had a little Spanish by this time and was able to tell them that I had been recently widowed and needed some time to myself. They were very sympathetic and were altogether lovely. It did me good to be with such simple, kindly people. I wondered if they would be so kind if they knew what I had done. It might have been all right. Spanish people had a reputation for believing in revenge. I didn't put it to the test, though.

The next day, I pushed on to Gandia. It was a very small place in those days, and down on the beach there were just two hotels – a small simple place at one end and, some way along the beach, another, more sophisticated one. A little further beyond the latter, a block of flats was going up. The show flat was already open, and I had a look. It was very nice, but I couldn't see that anyone would want to live in such a lonely out-of-the-way place. When I went to Gandia again, many years later, I couldn't find the little hotel, and the other was lost among the unending line of buildings spreading for miles along the coast. I couldn't move for holidaymakers, so it just goes to show what I knew about anything.

I made my way down the coast, trying to picture Laurie Lee walking the same route. I decided to make for Algeciras and see if I could get a room at the Reina Christina, a hotel I had read about. There was no problem as the season was over, and I settled into a delightful room overlooking the harbour. It was remarkably full of vessels. I had not realised that Algeciras was such a busy port. It was then that I got the idea of going over to North Africa but reluctantly decided that was a step too far on my own.

That evening, after dinner, I sat on the terrace with coffee and brandy and noticed a group of young people at a nearby table. They were a good-looking bunch. Healthy and happy looking. They were a bit drunk and quite loud, so it was not difficult to deduce that they were speaking with American accents. I decided to approach them and used the old trick of asking if they had a light – I smoked in those days and had a bag full of Bisonte Filtro. They were happy to oblige and invited me to join them. There were four of them, all college friends, and they were taking some time off after university, before entering the world of work – what we now call a 'gap year'. Teddy and John were big muscular young men and very alike to look at. The girls, Jenny and Sandy, were very different. Jenny was tall, long-limbed and slender, while Sandy was petite and pretty. They said that they were going over to Morocco, and I lay awake wondering whether they would mind if I joined them. I saw them at breakfast the next day and put it to them. I knew that they didn't have a car, and I offered to drive them if they didn't mind my going with them. I explained that I was dying to go over but was nervous of going alone. They were delighted and we went down to the ferry to book tickets. The boat looked as though it wouldn't make it across a duck pond, but we knew that the journey wasn't long, and the weather was calm.

I'd found Spain different and exotic, but Tangier was like being on another planet. The colours and the scents, the foreignness of the language. French was heard, but it was mainly what I took to be Arabic, and it sounded so romantic. I was still quite naïve, despite my previous horrific experiences, and still in the stage where I found camels, donkeys and people in robes fascinating. I had noticed poverty in Spain, and there was much evidence of it here, but it didn't seem like the poverty beneath the grey skies of England. I know better now, of course, but then it all seemed to take me back to biblical times and I loved it.

We didn't stay long in Tangier as Teddy's parents had booked a riad for them in Marrakesh. They invited me to stay with them and I gratefully accepted. They really were the nicest group of people I had ever met. Were all Americans like that? I wondered. Maybe my next husband would be American.

We arrived in Marrakesh new town and found somewhere to park. Teddy had the address of the agent, and my French came in handy. We stopped a local and he took us to the agent's office. He seemed to us to be unusually helpful, but we found everyone in Marrakesh was the same. Nothing was too much trouble. We later found that the laws of Islam make it obligatory to help the stranger. I have to say, though, that everyone we met was extremely friendly, whether it was their law or not. They were just nice people. Even the sellers in the souq who were trying to get money out of us.

The house was in the old town, the Medina, and we found we had to leave the car where we had parked and carry our luggage. We followed Karim, the agent, through empty, winding streets full of buildings that seemed to have no windows, just doors, until he stopped in front of one and handed us the key.

'Why are the streets deserted, Karim?' asked John.

'It is time to eat. In fact, you caught me only just in time. I was just closing to go to my home.'

'We're very sorry,' we chorused, 'we had no idea.'

He smiled, bowed, touched forehead, mouth and breast, and turned away. He was soon lost from sight.

We looked at each other in dismay; the house didn't seem very pleasant. However, when we opened the door and went in, we found how wrong we were. We entered a delightful courtyard with windows and doors leading to a number of rooms. There was a shady tree and many flowers in pots in the courtyard, and it turned out to be a pleasant place to sit in the heat of the day.

'Wow,' said Teddy, 'this is something like.'

The rooms– there were enough for one each – were equally lovely, with tiles, cushions, and beautiful tapestries on the walls. They were covered with colourful, geometric designs; no pictures of people or animals. We each chose a room. I hung back to let them have first choice, but in fact all the rooms were so nice that it wouldn't have mattered which one I chose. The kitchen had some basics, including bread and cheese, so we decided to eat then and go out later to look round.

Chapter 8

What a difference when we went out later. People were everywhere, heavily laden donkeys blocked the narrow streets, and the noise was deafening. We had a plan of the town, so headed for the main square. It was about five o'clock and the square was full of entertainers of one sort or another; musicians, dancers, snake charmers, jugglers. We didn't know where to look at first. In fact, we didn't get a chance straight away because as soon as we appeared in the square, we were surrounded by children chattering and holding out their hands. A man in robes and an Arab head-dress shooed them away. We were grateful at first, but then it appeared that he wanted to be our guide. He was closely followed by a number of others, jostling to get near us, and all apparently after the same thing.

We were just deciding to go back to the house when Karim appeared, as if by magic, and chased the would-be guides away. He smilingly waved away our thanks.

'This will happen every time you come out,' he said. 'Would you like me to select a guide for you? He will take you where you want to go and keep the others away. I will arrange a good price with him.'

We accepted gratefully, and he went to talk to the group of guides and came back with one whom he introduced as Said. He shook hands with John and Teddy but not with us girls. Karim explained that as a religious man, he could not touch a woman who was not related to him, but that as we were foreigners, he did not object to being seen with us. Jenny and Sandy were somewhat offended at this, but I pointed out that we would expect them to observe our customs in our countries, so we must do the same in theirs.

'So, where do you want to go first?' asked Said.

We were a little nonplussed as we had not really discussed this. I asked Said if there was a regular route, looking round the notable buildings, and he said there was, so I looked enquiringly at the others. They all nodded, and we arranged for Said to meet us at the house early the next morning.

'I hope that you will not be offended if I advise you.' He looked at us enquiringly. 'Advise is the correct word?'

We said that it was, wondering what was coming next.

'It would be best if the ladies covered their arms and the gentlemen,' here, he looked at the boys' legs, 'did not wear shorts. It will draw attention to us. You will notice that most men and all women wear traditional dress here.'

'Should we cover our heads?' I asked. He shook his head. 'That is not necessary, but a hat for the sun would be a good idea.' He thought for a moment and added, 'May I ask that you do not hold hands or touch each other in any way. This would be regarded as a great offence.'

We all laughed. 'Don't worry, Said, we are just friends. No hand-holding.'

'Before you go, Said, can you recommend somewhere we could eat this evening?'

'Come with me now and I will show you some suitable restaurants. Do you want French or local cuisine?'

'Local,' we chorused.

He smiled. 'Well, be careful what you eat. Make sure it is cooked, and well cooked at that. We are used to our cuisine, but you may get ill if you are not careful, and that would rather spoil your holiday.'

He showed us a number of eating places, and we chose one that was decorated with beautiful tilework. Said spoke to the proprietor, who smiled at us and said, in French, that he would save a special table for us. What this meant, we had no idea, but he seemed delighted to see us, so we arranged to return later. We decided to go back to the house and change into more suitable dress and returned at about nine o'clock to the restaurant.

Alcohol was not served, but we were given mint tea in abundance and little cakes to go with it. The main course arrived in strangely shaped pots, which we learnt were called tagines. They contained some sort of delicious-smelling stew. The proprietor, who said to call him Abdel, told us that his people would eat with their hands, taking pieces of meat from the tagine, but that he did not expect us to do that as we would burn ourselves. He provided us with spoons which we dipped into the pot. We were a little chary of putting the spoons in our mouths then back into the pot but soon got used to it.

The meat was delicious and so was the homemade bread. I would have liked a glass of wine with it, but the mint tea was surprisingly tasty and made a good contrast with the rich stew. We had some more, very sweet, cakes for dessert and had a thoroughly enjoyable evening.

The next morning, Said collected us at 7.30 and looked approvingly at our dress. By the end of the morning, we were exhausted. He took us to see what seemed to be every historic building in the city, although he assured us that there were many more. There were many amazing sights, but the Ali Ben Youssef Madrasa was very special. You enter via a narrow passage, and I felt disappointed when I saw the entrance. However, this opened out into a magnificent court full of tiles in geometric designs – no people, animals or plants again, as these were apparently regarded as Allah's province.

The next day we went to the souqs, where I bought a lovely rug. Said asked if we would like to go to the camel market, which was on that day. This sounded interesting, so we made our way to the square where it took place. It was filled with the smell and sound of these amazing animals. I had not realised how tall they were, or how haughty they look. I asked Said where they would go after being sold and was horrified to hear that they were to be slaughtered for meat. It was foolish, I suppose, but it had not occurred to me that camel meat was as normal in the Middle East as beef is to us.

'Was that camel we had last night?' asked Jenny, looking horrified.

'Yes, it was. But you enjoyed it, didn't you?'

We had to agree that we had, but we all felt a little odd to think that we had eaten of the meat of these lovely animals. For a while, we all thought of becoming vegetarians, I think, at least while we were in Morocco, but that didn't last long as we found that we could have sheep and goat and did not need to eat camel. We giggled a little shamefacedly over our hypocrisy, but I wouldn't have been happy eating horse, either.

Said then took us to the food market, which was wonderful. Full of colour and exotic scents. We bought enough food to feed an army. We dined in that night, and that is what started our problems.

After dinner, with which we had wine, Teddy produced what turned out to be marijuana. He had the impression that it was OK to smoke it in Morocco, and I must say that I had thought the same, although I had never smoked it before. When I was at university, we were still drinking alcohol, not doing drugs, and I was therefore a little scared about smoking it. However, the others assured me that they had been smoking for some time; that it had no bad effects and was very enjoyable. I was still wary and just had a couple of puffs, which didn't have any effect on me at all. I have never drunk to excess, either. I suppose I am something of a control freak, but I always like to be in charge of what I'm doing.

We were pretty sure that we had noticed the smell of it coming from neighbouring houses the night before. Maybe we did and maybe we made our mistake by going up onto the roof to smoke. The scent must have drifted next door, and the next day we were woken by banging on the door. When we opened it, two policemen pushed their way in and announced, in French, that we were under arrest. The others had no French, so I had to be the spokesman. I pointed out that we were foreign nationals and had not done anything wrong. They would not listen. They said we had been reported for dealing in hashish and that we would have to accompany them to the police headquarters.

Chapter 9

I explained what was happening to the others, and John started to bluster about being an American citizen and that his father was an important man. I stopped him and said that we had better do what they said and ask to see the American and British consuls.

They did not treat us roughly in any way, but nonetheless it was very frightening, as we did not know what was going to happen. We arrived at the police station and were put together into a small room, where we waited for what seemed like hours. We were then taken out, one at a time, and interviewed by what we took to be the chief of police. He said that we had been reported as dealing in hashish. We all told the same story, which was the truth, that we had smoked some marijuana which we had brought with us, and we had not realised that it was against the law. We thought that we would probably be fined and that would be that. In fact, we were locked up in the small room again and left there all night. The next day, we appeared in court. I explained to what I took to be the magistrate and asked that we see the American and British consuls.

It was difficult for us to work out what was going on as, although they spoke French to us and I translated for the others, the proceedings were conducted in Arabic. I could see that things were going against us, so I stood up again and demanded we have a lawyer. An order was given, and we were taken back to the police station and locked up in the same room. We were seriously frightened by now. After a while, the door was opened, the other four were taken away and I was left alone. Almost immediately after, a man in European clothes came in and introduced himself as being from the British Embassy. I was so relieved, I could have kissed him. However, he was not able to offer much comfort. Apparently, we had been found guilty in the court, and discussions were now going on as to what our punishment would be.

'I will do my best to ensure that you just get a fine, but there has been a clampdown on drug dealing lately,' he held up his hand as I began to protest, 'yes, I know you have not been dealing, you were just smoking it, but that's what they've decided.'

'So, what will happen now?'

'You will have to remain here while we get some discussions going behind the scenes. I'm sorry, I know it's not very pleasant here, but there's nothing else we can do. Her Majesty's Government does not have much influence here.'

After he had gone, the others were brought back. They had apparently had the same experience with their government's representative. They seemed to me to be feeling foolishly confident that Morocco would not want to have an international incident with the USA. I didn't tell them that I thought they were wrong, as I didn't want to bring their spirits down. My personal feeling, though, was that we would be made an example of, and I was not hopeful about the future. I had heard of people getting twenty-year sentences. My mind was working furiously. How could I work out which was the best person to bribe? If I tried to bribe the wrong person, then we could end up in an even worse position.

'Look,' I said, 'if the worse comes to the worst, we will have to try to bribe someone. The problem is, who?'

'We don't have enough money with us to bribe anyone,' said Teddy.

'Don't worry, I'll see to that. The problem is not knowing how the hierarchy works here. If I can work out who has any actual power, and is open to bribes, then we have a chance.'

'Our government will get us out,' said John. 'My father is an important person back home. They won't dare keep us here.'

'John, please, take my advice. This is not like the old days when a gunboat could be sent to free our nationals. This country is independent and has different views from ours. It could even be that we are caught up in some political matter that has nothing to do with us. We must just keep calm, don't shout at anyone, and don't try to throw our weight around, because we don't have any.'

The others agreed with me, and John subsided but was obviously not happy.

The sound of a key turning in the lock had us all looking at the door. It was a guard, who indicated that we should follow him. He would not answer questions. Perhaps he didn't understand any language but his own, but I had the impression that he had been instructed not to talk to us.

He led us to another part of the prison where we were separated; the boys in one room and Jenny, Sandy and me in another. The rooms adjoined, and we were able to hear each other talking but, as the walls were thick, not what was being said.

We looked round the room. There were three mattresses and that was all. I hammered on the door and a guard opened the spyhole.

'What if we need the toilet?' I asked in French.

He went away and came back a short time later with a bucket. Jenny and Sandy were outraged, and I asked if we

49

could have one each. The guard laughed and came back with two more.

'They can't treat us like this,' shouted Sandy angrily.

'No, but they are. You must know the story about the man who was sent to jail and when a friend came to see him and asked him what he had done said, "But they can't put you in jail for that." "No," said the man, "but they have." Look, girls, there is nothing we can do about it at this stage. Our embassies will do what they can. In the meantime, we can do nothing but wait. Make sure your watches are kept wound so that we know what time it is.'

We sat on our mattresses, which were not very clean, but there was nowhere else to sit. Jenny started to cry, and Sandy put her arm round her.

'Why did we come to this beastly country in the first place? We must have been mad.'

I was getting a little annoyed with them and said, rather sharply, 'How do you think I feel? I've never even smoked hash before and I'm in jail for drug dealing.'

'I'm sorry, Lily, I'm so sorry we've got you into this,' said Sandy.

'Never mind, let's look upon it as an adventure. When we get out of it, we'll have plenty to tell the folks back home.'

Jenny stopped crying and tried to smile.

'Yes, my family will never believe this. They don't even know I smoke hash.'

'Mine won't be surprised at all. They have been expecting something like this to happen to me for years,' said Sandy ruefully. 'I'll never hear the end of it.'

They were both more cheerful by now, and I felt I could devote my mind to working out what to do if I got the chance. I didn't really have a great deal of money with me, although I did have some jewellery, so bribery might be a slim chance, unless sexual favours would work. It was notorious that the men in this country had difficulty getting sex before marriage so perhaps that might work. That would be a last resort, though. I would rather use my brains than my body. I fell asleep trying to work out scenarios.

We were woken by the door being opened and a guard coming in with a tray. On it were some dates and bread and what turned out to be almond milk. We fell upon it hungrily and, little though it was, felt better for it. When the guard came for the tray, I asked him if there was somewhere we could wash. He pointed to the buckets and for a moment I thought he meant that we should wash in our own urine. However, he just wanted us to bring the buckets, and he led us to a yard where there was a drain and a tap.

We emptied the buckets and washed them out. He indicated that we should put water in the buckets to wash with. This we did not want to do, but the alternative was to strip and wash in front of him. We washed our faces at the tap and filled one of the buckets. We agreed that we would keep that one for washing water and share the other two. The guard led us back to our prison and, when he had gone, we washed as well as we could. We had no option but to put on our dirty clothes, but at least we felt a little cleaner.

We wondered how Teddy and John were doing. I put my ear to the wall to try to hear if they were talking. I took off my shoe and hit the wall with it and put my ear back. A knock came from the other side, so at least we knew that they were still there. Somehow, this made us feel better.

The man from the Consulate came again and said that they were not getting anywhere but would keep at it. He asked if he could bring us anything and was rather embarrassed, I think, when we asked for clean underwear. He said he would do what he could. The main thing he intended to do was to keep visiting us on a regular basis so that the police would know that we were not forgotten. We thanked him profusely. We all felt a little sad when he went; he was our only contact with the outside world.

At lunchtime, another tray was brought in, this time with bread, cheese and some more dates. The guard also brought a small table and three stools. It is amazing how little improvements make such a difference. We felt quite decadent sitting at a table, even though we were still eating with our fingers. On the other hand, I feared that it meant that we were to be kept here for some time, but I didn't mention it to the girls.

Later in the day, the guard came and took us outside. At first, we thought that we were to be released, but it was only for some exercise. We were dejected when we found out, but then the boys joined us, and we couldn't stop hugging and laughing with relief that we were all still alive. The guard shouted at us and made the boys go to the other side of the yard, but at least we were together for a while. Then we were led back to our cells and left alone until the evening meal. This was more filling as it consisted of a stew with more bread and some of those delicious little cakes. This cheered us as we thought they would not be looking after us so well if we had been forgotten by the outside world. Little did we know, as the old stories say.

We settled down for another night but did not sleep as well as we had the previous night, when we had been so tired. It was difficult not to fear what was to happen to us. Particularly as we had apparently already been tried and found guilty. Were we to spend years in this little cell?

Chapter 10

The next day, the man from the Consulate returned. He was smiling and our hearts lifted.

'Good news,' he said, 'they have decided to be lenient. You will each receive a sentence of nine months in prison.'

'In what way is that good news?'

'You don't understand, Lily, you could have got twenty years, but for some reason that I do not quite grasp, they have decided to go easy on you.'

'And will we have to spend nine months in this rotten little cell with no toilet facilities?'

'No, you will be moved to a proper prison with reasonable facilities. Mind you, it will not be as good as an English prison, but it will be much better than this. I will still visit you whenever I am allowed and will bring in anything you need.'

He turned to the other girls. 'I am sure that the American Consulate will do the same for you.'

'Well,' said Sandy, 'they don't seem to be doing much so far. We haven't seen our guy since that first time. Can you get in touch and find out what they are doing for us?'

'I will certainly speak to them and make sure they realise what is happening. I don't understand why they haven't visited you.'

When he had gone, we tried to work out how we felt about these latest developments. On the one hand, we didn't fancy spending nine months in prison; on the other hand, at least we now knew where we stood.

'It might be that our man is still trying to get us out of

here, so I'm not giving up yet,' said Jenny. 'Surely they won't leave us here to rot.'

'I'm not so sure,' replied Sandy. 'I don't think students are that popular with our authorities at the moment. They might think we deserve all we get.'

Jenny's face fell and Sandy put her arm round her.

'Never mind, Jenny, we're still together, and remember, Lily thinks she might be able to get us out of this.'

They both looked appealingly at me, and I tried to look reassuring, but really, I couldn't see what I could do. There was no use trying to bribe the guards. That might get us outside, but then what? I needed someone more senior.

I was sitting wondering what I could do to get us out when Jenny, who was using the bucket, suddenly gave a little scream.

'What is it, Jenny, what's the matter?' asked Sandy anxiously.

I was anxious too. Was Jenny having a breakdown? However, there seemed to be a good reason for her screaming.

'Someone was looking through the spyhole at me,' Jenny said when she could speak.

'Are you sure?'

'No, but I think I saw a light and then an eyeball. I always look at the door when I use the bucket. We know that they check on us every now and again, and I am frightened that they might see me.'

'Maybe your fear made it appear as though there was an eye there.'

'No, Lily, I really do think it was someone looking.'

'OK, next time one of us needs the bucket, one of us should stand to the side of the door and then have a quick look at the spyhole.'

'I could do with going now,' said Sandy.

I moved over to the door and stood silently and without moving.

'I don't know why I need to pee so much. It's not as though they give us much to drink,' said Sandy, picking up the bucket and putting it down noisily.

Jenny kept an eye on the door and, after a couple of minutes, signalled to me. I moved quickly and put my eye to the hole, where I looked straight into another eye on the other side. It was gone instantly but it had definitely been there. How many times had we been spied on in this way? We all felt violated, and it was some time before we could calm down.

When the guard brought in our next meal, I asked if I might see the captain. He said he would ask, but he didn't think I could. While we waited for a reply, the time went very slowly. We kept looking at our watches and wondering if they were right. No one came near us, and we had to spend another night on the dirty mattresses. It was cold too. I hadn't expected it to be cold in Morocco, but at night the temperature dropped alarmingly. On the first night, we had decided to push the mattresses together so that we could cuddle together for warmth. We wondered if the boys were doing the same, and this made us giggle, which in turn made us feel better.

When the breakfast was brought the next morning, the guard said that the captain would be coming that day and that I could have an interview with him. He seemed ill at ease, and I wondered if he was the one who had been spying on us. I thought that he understood French and thought I would try to enlist him on our side.

'I know what you have been doing,' I said, pointing at the spyhole. He blanched and said that it wasn't him but one of the other guards.

'How do you know what I am talking about then?'

He said nothing but looked scared.

'I won't say anything if you will help us.'

'What can I do? I have no power here.'

'Could you get us a blanket? We get very cold at night.'

He grinned. 'I know, one of the night guards watches you all lying together.'

I slapped his face, and he turned red with embarrassment and anger.

'I will tell the captain when he gets here unless you get us a blanket and some more food and drink. We are starving.'

He glowered at me, but I could tell that I had the upper hand.

'I'll do what I can,' he muttered, and left the cell.

The girls looked at me impatiently. 'What was all that about?' asked Sandy.

'First things first. He says that the captain is coming and that he will see me. The rest was about him getting us a blanket and some more food. I don't know if he will manage it, but at least I may now have a chance of bribing the captain.'

'What will you bribe him with, do you have a lot of money with you?'

'No, but I do have some gold jewellery, and I could always give him the car.'

'I thought the car was on hire in Spain,' said Jenny.

Sandy looked at her pityingly. 'What does that matter if it gets us out of here? We can sort that out later.'

'Yes, I may be able to claim on the insurance, say it was stolen or something. I'll worry about that if we get out of this country.'

Chapter 11

We didn't sleep much that night, and when the breakfast was brought in, we asked the guard what time the captain would get there. Unfortunately, he was one of those who spoke neither English nor French, and he just looked at us and went out.

We ate in silence, each lost in our own thoughts. I was trying to remember what the captain was like. Did he seem the sort who would take a bribe, and if so, how big a bribe would he need? He was a handsome man, if it turned out to be the same man, and probably vain, which might help.

The morning dragged on. Lunch came, and still no sign of the captain. We began to lose heart then, without warning, the door opened, and the guard pointed to me and beckoned for me to follow him.

'Wish me luck, girls.' They both gave me the thumbs-up, and I followed the guard out of the cell, down the corridor and into the interview room that we had been taken to on the first day. The captain was sitting behind the desk. He rose as I came in, which I took to be a good sign.

'Please be seated, Mrs Antrobus. I hope that you are being treated properly?'

'We have not been ill-treated in any way, Captain, but we have not been comfortable, as I am sure you will appreciate.'

He smiled and sat down again himself.

'I am sure that prisoners in any jail in any country are not comfortable, Mrs Antrobus, but I will see what I can do.'

'Blankets would be helpful; it gets really cold at night. We found that very surprising as we thought of Morocco as a very warm country.'

'I think many foreigners have a number of misconceptions about Morocco,' he replied dryly. 'However, you wanted to see me. Was it about the blankets, or do you wish to know where you will be moved to from here?'

I took a deep breath. *Here goes*, I thought.

'I wanted to see you to discuss where we will go from here certainly, but I rather hoped that we might be able to work out something that enables us to go home.'

'That will be very difficult, Mrs Antrobus. The court has already found you guilty.'

'So I understand, but that hardly seems fair when we did not know what was going on in court and were not allowed to defend ourselves. I for one have never been involved in taking drugs, and I am sure that none of the others have been drug dealing. They may have a little cannabis for their own use but that is all.'

'I don't know how much power you think I have, Mrs Antrobus, but once the court has spoken, there is nothing I can do.'

'I think you rather underestimate your powers, Captain. I am sure that if you were to exercise yourself on our behalf, much could be achieved. I do appreciate that you would have to compensate various people, and I hoped that we could come to some arrangement whereby this could be done.'

He looked thoughtfully at me. 'It is not impossible that something might be done, but as you say, there will be a number of people who would need to be compensated, as you put it. How is this to be achieved?'

'I don't think that the others have much money. They are only students, and I do not have a great deal of cash with me.

However, I do have with me some gold jewellery. I must tell you, Captain, that I was widowed less than a year ago and my husband was very rich. Unfortunately, he had been married before and had a family, so most of his money went to them. However, he was a very generous man and bought me some very valuable jewels. As these were gifts, they belong to me.'

'And do you have all these valuable jewels with you?' he asked, looking unconvinced.

'Not all of them, obviously, but I did bring some, which I hid in the car. I don't know why I brought them with me really. I suppose I thought I might meet some people and go to expensive restaurants where I would dress up and put on my jewels. As it happens, the people I met turned out not to have much money at all and were not interested in dressing up and going out. The pieces I brought with me must be worth quite a bit. Obviously, not what they cost, but their weight in gold alone should bring a reasonable amount. Some of them are set with precious stones, which could perhaps be taken out and sold separately. I also have the car.'

'But the car is on hire, is it not?'

'Yes, that is true, and I would have some difficulty when I got back to Spain, but I am sure that I could sort that out, and it will be worth whatever trouble is caused if we can get back home.'

'Why are you concerned about the others? You have not known them long.'

'I am concerned because they are young, innocent people, and they have been very kind to me. We met in Algeciras, and they allowed me to join them and have given me hospitality in their house. I am sure that you, Captain, can understand that I feel obliged to them.'

'Yes, I do understand but am surprised to find that your culture also obeys the laws of hospitality.'

'We may have more in common than we think, Captain.'

He looked at me speculatively, and I began to feel more confident.

'Leave this with me, Mrs Antrobus, and I will make some enquiries and see what I can do.'

I stood up and held out my hand. He rose also and taking my hand did not shake it but raised it to his lips. I felt even more confident and smiled demurely at him.

He called for the guard who took me back to the cell, where the girls were waiting eagerly.

'How did it go, what did he say?'

'Give me a chance, let me get in.'

I waited until I heard the guard go away and then told them what had happened.

'Do you think anything will come of it?' asked Jenny.

'It is difficult to say, but I do feel more optimistic now.'

We sat down at the table and started to make plans of what we would do when we got out. I thought it would be best if we all flew out at the earliest opportunity, to give no time for people to change their minds. The girls thought so too. When our evening meals were brought, there was another guard carrying blankets and pillows. When he had gone, the first guard took a loaf from his jacket.

'This was the best I could do,' he said, and we smiled in gratitude.

We thought these were good signs and we slept better that night.

Chapter 12

I waved Jenny, Sandy, John and Teddy off as they walked to the plane. They were so relieved and grateful they had pledged eternal friendship and promised to write to me as soon as they got home. No doubt they would write, but I was sure that they would soon forget. They were only human, and they were very young. I may have been only seven years older than them, but I had much more experience of life and I had become cynical.

In fact, I was wrong. They did remember, and we were penfriends for years. They even came to see me in London the following year and, years later, I went to America and met their spouses and children. It was good to know that there were some nice people in the world, particularly when it also contains people like me.

'Right,' I said, turning to the captain, 'when can I have my passport?'

'Soon, it is at my little hideaway. We will go there now and get it, but first, where is the gold? Give me that and then perhaps we can have a meal and then tomorrow I will drive you to the airport to get your plane back to England.'

'It is hidden in the car. I'll get it now.'

We returned to the car, and I fished the package out of its hiding place and handed it to him.

'How will you explain to the insurance company about the car?'

'I don't know, I'll think of something. If I say it was stolen, they will expect a police report. Could you give me one?'

'I'm sure something can be arranged. Come on, let us go and eat.'

We drove back into town, and he took me to a charming little restaurant where we had an excellent meal and some equally excellent wine. I was feeling very relaxed when we started out for his apartment. Relaxed, but still wary. It was pretty obvious that I was not going to get away without having sex with him. I didn't mind that; he was a good-looking man, but I was still not sure that he would keep his side of the bargain and give me back my passport.

The apartment was within walking distance of the restaurant, so we left the car in the side street where he had parked it. The building was not very impressive, but once we got inside the apartment itself, I gasped, much to his amusement. It was luxurious and surprisingly tasteful. The wall hangings were traditional rugs, and there were traditional objets d'art dotted about. The furniture, however, was western and very comfortable. The apartment wasn't large – a living room, bedroom, kitchen and shower room – but it was beautifully appointed, and I realised that he must have been taking bribes for a long time.

He held up a decanter. 'A nightcap?' I nodded and he poured two glasses of what I took to be cognac. It was, and very good cognac at that. I wandered round the room, looking at the carved figures and photographs on the shelves. The photographs were all of lovely women, some disturbingly young-looking.

'Are these all your conquests?' I asked, pointing at the pictures.

He smiled in an arrogant manner. 'Just some of them, look here,' and he handed me a photograph album. I turned the pages and there were pictures of lovely women in various stages of undress, some completely naked. On the next page, the women in the photos seemed to be asleep, and I was about to remark on this, when he took the book from me and replaced it on the shelf.

He held up the decanter and I shook my head.

'It is very late, why don't you spend the night here? It will be difficult to find a hotel at this time of night.'

'You said that my passport was here, but I haven't seen any sign of it.'

He went into the bedroom and came back with my passport. 'Here it is,' he said, and put it down on the table. I picked it up and checked it. It was mine and seemed to be all in order.

'You have a very suspicious mind,' he said, laughing.

He came across, took my hand and raised it to his lips, but instead of kissing the back he turned it over and kissed the palm. I felt an electric shock run through me. I felt quite happy; this was going to be fun, I'd get my passport back and then I could go home. He led me to the bedroom, kissing and caressing me very gently. We took off our clothes and got onto the bed and began to make love.

It was fine for a while, then he began to get a little rough. I put my hand on his shoulder and tried to push him away, but he put his hands around my throat.

'Not another one!' I thought. 'What do I do now?'

I decided I could do nothing about it; he was much stronger than me, so I would just lie there until he finished. The problem was, he was tightening his grip on my throat; I was having difficulty breathing. I hit his shoulder and tried to speak but couldn't form words, just a croaking sound. I thought that would get through to him, but then I looked at his face. I don't quite know how to describe it; it was as though he wasn't there. He had turned into an automaton, and the grip was getting tighter and tighter.

The panic that I'd been feeling disappeared, and my mind clicked into what I can only call survival mode. I tried to get my knee between his legs, but he was too heavy on top of me. I reached out with my hand to see if there was something on the bedside table I could use as a weapon, and it closed on the bedside lamp. I slid my hand up to the top, swung it with what little strength I had left and managed a lucky blow to his head. He immediately passed out.

I lay for a while trying to get my breath back. My lungs were heaving like bellows. My heart was pounding, my pulse racing. Gradually, I calmed down and I could breathe again, but I still had this deadweight on top of me. I managed to roll him off me onto the other side of the bed and lay for another couple of minutes, my mind racing. I had to get out of here before he came to. I set up on the edge of the bed and looked round. Was there something I could tie him up with?

I turned and looked at him and realised for the first time that he didn't seem to be breathing. My nerves had returned by this time, and I didn't want to touch him.

I imagined him suddenly coming to and grabbing hold of me again. I gritted my teeth, got up, went round to the other side of the bed and tried to feel his pulse. I couldn't feel anything, but the pulse in the wrist is often difficult to get. I put my ear to his chest and couldn't hear any heartbeat. He was dead.

I couldn't believe that that one blow to his head had killed him. It was a heavy lamp, certainly, but I hadn't been able to get any power behind the blow. It must've been a combination of the weight of the lamp itself and where the blow landed.

This opened up a completely new line of thought. I could just go, drive to Tangier, get the boat back to Spain. But what if they found his body before I got there? I didn't know whether he'd told anyone that he was going to take me to his flat. It didn't seem likely, if he intended to kill me, and if he had already killed the girls in those photographs, he would want to keep it quiet, but you can never tell with psychopaths.

Even so, it would look strange. I had to make it look like an accident. I would drag him into the shower and make it look as though he'd slipped and banged his head. He was already naked, so I didn't have to take his clothes off. He was quite a heavy man, but my strength had returned now, and I managed to get him off the bed onto the floor and was able to pull the rug across to the shower room with him on it. I got him into the shower, pulled the rug out from underneath him and replaced it. I then turned the shower on so that he was wet, put shampoo on his head and left the shower running.

I dressed quickly, wiped all the surfaces I could think of that I had touched, picked up my passport and packet of jewellery and left. I pulled my scarf round my head, hiding as much of my face as I could and, keeping close to the wall, made my way back to the car.

I drove through the night to Tangier and got the first boat the next morning. I didn't relax until I was back in Spain. Even then, I kept expecting to be picked up by the police and sent back to Morocco, and it wasn't until I got on the plane at Barcelona that I really breathed easily.

For the next couple of weeks, I watched the papers for anything concerning the captain's death and the English woman being sought by the police, but nothing appeared. I even managed to get French editions of a Moroccan paper, but there was nothing about it. Once again, I had got away with it. I began to believe that I was leading a charmed life.

Chapter 13

Once back in England, I lived a quiet life for a while, just going out to buy essential food or for a walk around the park. After all the excitement in Morocco, that was all I wanted. But of course, after a few months, I wanted a change.

I now decided that I deserved a nice holiday. Using my maiden name, I obtained a new passport and travelled to the French Riviera. I booked into a hotel a little down the coast from Nice, not the fashionable part but the quieter area of the coast while I got my bearings. I took the most expensive room at a hotel at the end of the promenade and spent a quiet few weeks recovering from the stress of recent months.

Feeling refreshed, I decided to move to Nice, where the money was, and found an apartment in the most fashionable quarter and established myself with the various authorities. I dressed to kill, in a ladylike way, of course, and went for a walk along The Promenade des Anglais. I had by now taught myself to move with confidence and with an air. It isn't difficult when you have got away with murder. I wasn't over-confident, though. I knew that I would never be entirely safe, but safe enough. Having money makes you feel even safer.

While I gave the impression of being interested only in the sea and sky, I was in fact scoping out where the richest people seemed to congregate. I decided on a particular café and sat down. A waiter immediately appeared and, in English, I ordered a coffee.

There was an attractive group at a nearby table, youngish middle-age, the women very smart and the men good-looking. They began to talk about me in rapid French. I couldn't get all the words but enough to get the meaning and decided to try to make contact. I turned my head sharply towards them, making it obvious that I understood, and they looked away in embarrassment. I turned my head back and looked at the sea again and became aware that one of the men was standing beside me.

'I do apologise, mademoiselle; we were very remiss. We made assumptions about your ability to understand French. It was very rude of us. Please forgive us.'

He smiled down at me. He had a very pleasant smile, warm and friendly. I laughed up at him.

'Not at all, monsieur, it was most amusing,' I replied in my best French.

'At least let us buy you a drink. Won't you join us?'

I rose and crossed to their table. The men rose to their feet, smiling and bowing. The women smiled, although not so convincingly, and we all introduced ourselves.

'A glass of wine perhaps?'

'Thank you, but it is a little early for me and I have already ordered a coffee – and here it is.'

I signalled to the waiter, who was standing by my original table looking annoyed. Then he saw me, was mollified, and brought the coffee over. He didn't exactly smile – French waiters never smile – but he stopped frowning.

Through this fortunate contact, I made my way into local society and, in a purely academic way, started weighing up the men in the group to see if any of them were sufficiently interesting to consider as husband number three. None of them were, though. I could afford to be fussier than in the past, and anyway I had learnt my lesson with Jonathan. Charm isn't everything. They were a pleasant enough crowd to spend several days and evenings with, but they were pretty empty-headed. I had been spoiled by Charlie and Jonathan for uncultured men.

Life continued pleasantly enough. I thought I was untouchable, until one day I had an extremely unpleasant surprise. The private detective I had hired in England turned up. How he had managed to track me down, I don't know, and he didn't volunteer any information.

The first I knew of it was one evening at the casino. I was there with a group and placing a few bets in a desultory way – gambling has never been one of my vices. My lifestyle was enough of a gamble for me. If the truth be told, I was getting bored with my new friends. I was thinking of moving on and looking for something more interesting when my gaze was arrested by what I thought was a familiar face. I couldn't place it at first, then it suddenly struck me; it was Bob James, the private detective I had hired. A cold fear took hold of me. I did my best not to show it, but one of my companions looked at me with concern and asked if I was feeling ill.

'No, I'm fine, just a bit of a headache. I think I'll call it a night if no one minds.'

Everyone was concerned and full of advice, and several offered to see me home. Louis and Marianne, a couple with whom I had become very friendly, insisted on accompanying me and I accepted gratefully. I didn't feel up to being confronted by this face from the past. He had clearly seen me and had smiled in what seemed to me to be a sinister way.

Later, nursing a glass of Cognac, I tried to decide what to do. I didn't want to just run away. If he had found me once, he could probably do so again. I decided to wait and see if he contacted me. He might, after all, have been at the casino by coincidence. Even private detectives have holidays. I didn't really believe this, though, so I wasn't surprised when he turned up at the apartment the next evening. He must have followed us home on the previous night. I tried to look unconcerned.

'I thought it was you in the casino last night. What on earth are you doing down here? Business must be good if you can afford to holiday here.'

I indicated that he should come in. He smiled, walked in and sat down without being invited. His confidence worried and annoyed me.

'I'm here on business, but I hope to have a holiday afterwards.'

I asked if he would have a drink and he said he would have whatever I was having, so I poured him a generous Cognac and sat down opposite him. He looked round appreciatively.

'You've certainly landed on your feet. This is nice, very nice. I would like a place like this myself.'

'Well ... maybe one day,' I replied, speaking with a brightness I did not feel. It took all my acting ability, but I managed to sound and, I hoped, look happy and confident.

'Maybe one day soon,' he replied with a leer. 'Let's cut the cackle,' he said, 'you probably have a good idea why I'm here.'

'Not at all. I have been wondering what brought you here. Not to Nice, everyone ends up here eventually, but to my apartment. Our business was over a long time ago.'

'Not so. You didn't enquire how I managed to get you off the hook, and that's fair enough, but now I think you ought to know.'

'Is that necessary? You managed it and I was grateful, as my payment should have told you.'

He laughed. 'Oh yes, the payment. Did you really think I would settle for a measly fifty thousand with what I had found out?'

'I can't imagine that anything you found out affects me.'

'Not even that I know who bought the aphrodisiac that killed your husband? That I know that you went and picked it up?'

'That's preposterous. My husband ordered it himself and collected it himself. The man at the shop said it was a man.'

'Yes, but when I questioned him, he said he wasn't sure that it was a man. It could have been a woman dressed up.'

'Then why didn't he say that at the time?'

'Because people in a shady business never tell the police anything but the obvious, and, anyway, they respect their client's privacy.'

I laughed in what I hoped was a relaxed and scornful manner and took a sip of my drink.

'Are you trying to tell me that somebody who works in a shop of that kind has a sort of professional attitude, like a doctor?'

'No, not quite that, but they do play their cards very close to their chest. They never know when the little extra information that they possess may come in useful. And they are quite right, because it has come in useful. I paid him for the information and now I have what I need, so it is you who will pay me.'

'You have nothing. Jonathan could have got anyone to collect it for him. He wasn't the sort of man who'd go himself. Anyway, why on earth would I want to poison him, even assuming that I knew about such things?'

'Because, my dear, your husband turned out to be violent. I did some digging and I found out that his previous wife had also shown evidence of being beaten up, although she never admitted it.

'I visited the hospital where you were taken, and the doctor who treated you told me that he was convinced you had been physically assaulted, although you said you had fallen down the stairs.'

'Doctors would never reveal such things,' I said scornfully.

'You'd be surprised what people tell you when you approach them in the right way. I gave him the impression that you had changed your mind and wanted to bring a case against your husband. He didn't know that he was already dead, of course, and said that he would be willing to give evidence if you went to see him and told him yourself.'

I thought about this for a while. He could clearly make life very difficult for me, particularly if he teamed up with Jonathan's daughter. I made one last throw of the dice.

'What if it did come out that I had ordered the aphrodisiac? I didn't know it would kill Jonathan.'

'Maybe not, but how would it look? You having denied that you had anything to do with it and then it came out that you did. What would the daughter make of that?'

'OK. You have a point. So, what is it that you want? I'm not saying that there's anything in any of this, though. As far as I'm concerned, my life at that time is over, and I don't want it dragged up again. I'm prepared to pay you a reasonable amount to go away.'

'I've been doing some investigations into your financial position, and I reckon you could give me a million without too much trouble.'

I gasped. 'A million! Are you mad? There's no way I could give you a million.'

'Of course you could. Yes, it would make a big hole in your bank account, but you can easily find yourself another rich husband.'

I thought for a while. What he said was true, of course, but I didn't want to get married again just yet and, anyway, I wasn't going to let this cheap huckster beat me. How could I stall him?

'If you know so much about my financial position, you will know that I cannot come up with such a huge sum just like that. Shares or property will have to be sold. Anyway, how would I explain it to my financial advisor?'

'I have every confidence in you. You're a clever girl. You'll find a way.'

He smiled and leant back in a confident manner. He clearly thought he had the whip hand, and I couldn't deny that he did. I decided to appear to give in, for the time being anyway.

'I suppose I could say the money was to invest in property over here. I only rent this place.'

'That's it, now you're thinking.'

I got up and crossed to the drinks cupboard and poured myself another Cognac. I held up the decanter and looked at him and he held up his glass. I topped it up then sat down again and sipped thoughtfully.

'Where are you staying?'

He looked round. 'I thought I could stay here; you have plenty of room.'

'No, that wouldn't do at all. We mustn't be seen together. I am quite well in with the society set here and will have to look among them for my next meal ticket. If I'm seen about with a good-looking younger man, it will spoil my chances. Ideally, you should find a hotel further down the coast, and I will come to you when we need to meet.'

He was clearly pleased at being called good-looking. I smiled inwardly. This would be easy.

'Do I look stupid? What's to stop you flitting?'

'Two main things. First, as I said, I have a position here and don't want to have to start again somewhere else, and

72

second, you are pretty good at finding people, so I would never be able to relax. You will just have to trust me. And, don't forget, I am going to have to trust you not to come after me for more money.'

He rose to his feet and held his glass towards me. I stood up and we clinked glasses.

'Right, that's a deal. I'll find somewhere not too close and ring you when I am settled in. Give me your number.'

I wrote my number down, saw him out and sat down to think. I was damned if I was going to give him any of my hard-earned money. There was only one way to deal with him. He would regret tangling with me; I would see to that.

Chapter 14

He rang the next day with the address of his hotel, and I arranged to meet him that evening at a bar by the sea. I dressed with particular care, sexy but not too obvious, and I could tell by his appreciative glance that I was on the right track. He had ordered a bottle of champagne, which I do not particularly like but I pretended to be pleased.

'Had any further thoughts?' he asked.

'I've put things in train. I rang my man of business and told him that I wanted to invest in property down here. I pointed out that it was a boom business, and I had the chance of buying into some apartments in a block just going up. He thought it was a good idea but wanted more details and something in writing. I'm getting something on paper and will get some plans from one of the development companies.'

'Very good. You don't waste time, I'm glad to see.'

'What's the point? It has to be done, and I want to get it all over with as soon as possible. Meanwhile, we might as well try and be civilised about it.'

He raised his glass. 'I couldn't agree more. There's no need for us to be at odds. It is just a matter of business.'

We spent a pleasant evening together. I said I would keep him in touch with what was going on and we parted on friendly terms. He clearly thought that he had me under control and was lowering his guard. I went to see him again two days later, this time during the afternoon, and I took my bathing things with me. He was surprised, but I explained that I had been told that the swimming was particularly pleasant there and thought I would take advantage of it.

'I'll join you, if you have no objections.'

I smiled pleasantly. 'Not at all, I'll be glad of the company.'

This fitted in with my plans perfectly. I don't know what he had in mind, but I knew what my intentions were. I was going to persuade him into a relationship and try to make him think he had the chance of acquiring a rich trophy wife. If this meant sex, then I was quite looking forward to it. I was feeling the need after a long period of abstinence, and he was an attractive man. Besides, many female insects have sex with their mate before devouring him. We dined at a discreet little restaurant and afterwards walked along the promenade in the moonlight.

'It's getting late,' I said. 'Perhaps I should be getting back.'

'Are you sure you're fit to drive?'

'Possibly not, but I'll drive slowly and, anyway, what's the alternative?'

'You could stay at my place.'

This was going to be easy; men are such suckers.

'What are you suggesting, sir?' I said coquettishly.

In reply, he put his arms around me and kissed me gently, then more firmly. I pulled away a little then sank against him and kissed him passionately. It felt good. We walked back to his hotel and made our way to his room. I made sure that no one was around who could later report seeing us together. By the time we reached his room, we were tearing each other's clothes off and falling onto his bed, and I was immediately ready when he entered me. Afterwards, we lay there panting, then I began to laugh. He lit two cigarettes and handed me one. He really was predictable. I took it, although I don't usually smoke after sex.

"That was quite something, if a little short.'

I agreed but pointed out that we had the night before us. He caressed my body, and I could tell that it wouldn't be long before we would start again. I felt wonderful. I hadn't realised how much I was missing sex.

After that, we spent a lot of time together, always ending up in his bed, and I was pretty sure that he trusted me now. It was time to put my plan into action. I had purchased some rat poison a few days before, and I intended to find a way of putting it into his drink.

I suggested a moonlight picnic and swim and he agreed enthusiastically. The following night, we made our way to a secluded part of the beach, and he opened the inevitable bottle of champagne. While he searched the picnic basket for the pâté, I slipped some of the poison into his glass. We ate and drank then lay on the sand, an apparently happy couple.

After a while, I suggested a swim. He demurred, saying that he had indigestion.

'Come on, you big girl's blouse, race you!'

I pulled at his hand and ran into the sea, and he had no alternative but to follow me. We plunged in and I swam out, with him after me. After a while, I heard him gasp and I turned around. He was clutching his stomach and looked terrified.

'What is it?'

'I don't know, I have terrible pains,' he managed to say, then he screamed and sank beneath the water.

I made a show of trying to save him but in fact I was holding him under until I was sure he was dead. Then I swam back to shore, packed everything except for his clothes and made my way to my car. I drove back to Nice, elated that I had overcome yet another obstacle.

I watched the local papers over the next few days and at

last there was a report of a body found by a fisherman and of clothes found on the beach. The hotel had reported him missing as he owed them money, and the police were able to piece together who he was. It was just another tragic accident. The coroner brought in a verdict of accidental drowning and that was that, or so I thought.

Chapter 15

The winter season started, and the English set started to appear. They seemed pretty much like the French set; well heeled but empty-headed in the main. Pleasant enough but addicted to parties and gambling. A few of them spoke French after a fashion. Others would have refused to speak it even if they could. I acted as a sort of bridge between the two sets, and this enabled them to get together more than they had in previous years. Various liaisons started up across the divide, and a good time was had by all.

I was quite happy to spend the winter there with them, but matters were taken out of my hands. One night, I arrived back at the flat and found a strange man making himself very comfortable, sitting in a chair with a glass in his hand. I made a superhuman effort and managed to hold back a scream. Trying to look as much in control as possible, I advanced to the middle of the room.

'Who the hell are you and what are you doing in my flat?'

He smiled. 'Bob said you were good, and he was right.'

'Bob? Bob who?'

'Come on, darling, don't give me all that moody. Bob James. He and I are, or rather were, partners. I was the one Mrs Barber hired. Bob and I decided that we could make more by convincing her that there was nothing suspicious about her father's death and seeing what more we could get out of you. Then you disappeared, and it took Bob some time to find you.

'He came down here and everything seemed to be going well, when he suddenly stopped contacting me. I smelled a rat, so I came down to find out what was going on. Imagine my surprise when I find out that he had drowned. Fortunately, he had given me your address, so here I am. I don't know how you managed it. Bob was no fool, but you had better not try it on with me.'

I bit my lip and looked down. 'Do you mean to say that Bob was just using me? I thought there was something between us.'

He smiled but didn't speak, so I let some tears run down my cheeks.

'I can't tell you how terrible these last weeks have been. We went for a midnight swim and got separated in the dark. I searched frantically for him but couldn't find him. I came back here, not knowing what to do. I hoped against hope that he had made it to shore. I couldn't contact his hotel as no one knew we even knew each other, and I didn't want to get involved in a scandal.'

I realised that I was making no impression at all so gave it up.

'What do you want?'

'I want what Bob arranged with you. A million. How far along are you with that?'

'I've instructed my accountant to sell some shares and property, and I think that is nearly done.'

'Right, then tomorrow I will come back, and you can ring him and hurry him up.'

'Can't we meet somewhere else? I have a position to keep up here, and I don't want people to see a strange man coming to my home.'

'Oh no, you're not going to snow me the way you did Bob. He was the sentimental type, I'm not.'

'No, I can see that.'

I stood up and picked up the decanter. I filled my glass

and walked across to where he was sitting. I held the decanter up enquiringly and he held up his glass. I dropped the decanter and threw the contents of my glass in his face and ran for the kitchen. He was temporarily blinded, and I managed to reach the kitchen, grab a knife and was pretending to try to open the back door when he caught up with me. I waited until he put a hand on my shoulder then I whirled round and plunged the knife into his chest. I was lucky. It penetrated his heart and with a look of surprise he fell to the floor. He must have died instantly because when I checked his pulse it had stopped.

I walked unsteadily into the sitting room and sat down. I thought quickly, going over my options. I would have to ring the police. It was the only thing to do. I washed his glass and put it away then picked up the receiver.

They arrived remarkably quickly. I suppose the upmarket address galvanised them. I told them that I had arrived home to find a strange man in my flat, that I had tried to escape through the kitchen but couldn't get the door open in time. I said I had grabbed a kitchen knife, hoping to keep him off, but that he was running after me and ran straight onto the knife.

They at first thought it was a crime of passion, but my story was so convincing, and the state of the flat chimed with what I had said happened, so I was not arrested. There were a lot of formalities over the next couple of weeks, of course, and the case made all the papers. I couldn't go anywhere without being pursued by reporters, so I got permission from the police to move up the coast for a while.

The verdict was self-defence, and I was left without a stain on my character, legally at least. Unfortunately, the whole scandal ruined my position with the upper set. At first, everyone wanted to see me to get the juicy details, but when they found that there weren't any, they soon lost interest and started to see me as unlucky to know. One by one, they drifted away.

It was time to move on.

Chapter 16

Back in my cosy flat in London, I found that I was more shaken by my recent experiences than I would have expected. I decided to lie low for a while and went out only when really necessary. I had groceries delivered and watched TV a lot. I couldn't seem to get my brain round anything demanding. I disconnected the phone by the simple expedient of taking the receiver off the hook.

After about a week of living like a hermit, I decided to at least be open to the possibility of seeing someone by putting the phone back into action. No one rang. Who was I expecting? I thought to myself. Then, a couple of days later, it did ring and I leapt to answer it. It was Vickie.

'Where on earth have you been? I've been trying to get you for ages.'

'I've been away visiting relatives. Why have you been trying to reach me? Something interesting, I hope,' I said, in what I hoped was a bright, friendly voice.

'Joyce is down here for a few days, and we are all getting together on Friday evening for a meal. Do say you can come.'

I thought for a moment. I'd like to see Vickie, and Joyce was OK, but who else might be there? I decided to take the risk.

'I'd love to. Where are we going?'

Vickie named a restaurant and the time we were to meet, and I was left to decide what to wear. I was much richer than any of them, and my clothes showed it. I didn't want to appear to be showing off. I could hardly wear any of my 'sin and sangria' clothes, so I would have to do a little shopping.

I was surprised to find that I was quite excited at the prospect of seeing old college friends again. Even though I hadn't finished my degree, I had happy memories of my time at university.

Everyone was there when I arrived, and I was greeted with some enthusiasm, although someone said, 'Here's Lily, making an entrance as usual.' It was said without malice, however, and we all laughed. The usual greetings came next, followed by ordering of drinks, and we gradually settled down and were able to find out what we were all up to.

No one mentioned the deaths of my husbands, so I raised the matter myself. I told them how lovely Charlie had been and how Jonathan had turned out not to be as nice as I had thought. I didn't go into detail, but they were sympathetic.

'You must be worth a bob or two,' said Joyce, a little enviously, I thought.

'Well, I did all right, but you must remember that both Charlie and Jonathan had families, so most of their estates went to them, which is only right. I have got a lovely little flat in Mayfair, though. We must have a get-together there some time.'

I didn't really mean it, but they were all so enthusiastic that I resigned myself to seeing them all again. I invited them all to lunch on the following Sunday, and we parted assuring each other that we would not lose touch again.

In those days, Sunday lunch was still the traditional roast but, as I was not much of a cook at that time, I arranged for the chef of a well-known restaurant to cater for me. The girls were very impressed with the flat and the lunch, and I think there was definitely a bit of envy. They didn't show it, though, and I suppose they were consoling themselves with the thought that I was on my own and was, in a way, 'tainted goods', having had two husbands die on me. The meeting with the girls unsettled me. I realised that not having a purpose was not good enough for me. I began to think again about going back to university. Would it be possible, and if so, how would I fit in with the younger students? I was now in my late twenties; they would all be eighteen to twenty-one. I decided to write to my old tutor and see what he thought.

A couple of weeks later, I got a telephone call from him. He suggested I go and see him to discuss the possibilities.

'You think it may be possible then?'

'I think we might be able to work something out but—'

I interrupted him. 'I won't need a grant or any financial help.'

'I wasn't thinking about that aspect of it; it's a matter of places on the course that you were on originally. It might not be possible but there are other possibilities, so when can you come and see me?'

'At any time to suit you; my time is my own.'

We arranged for me to go to his office on the following morning. I felt quite excited about it and wondered what the 'other possibilities' might be. They turned out to be a total surprise and affected my life for the next two years.

Alex, my tutor, greeted me with pleasure. He had always been impressed by my facility with language and had very much regretted that I had to leave university without completing my degree. After the usual greetings and enquiring what we had each been doing, he poured two cups of coffee, offered me the sugar, which I declined, and leant back in his chair.

'So, what of these other possibilities?'

'Since we spoke, I have been enquiring about the course that you were on before, and it might just be possible to squeeze you in. But I have a suggestion which might be of more interest to you. How good is your French, by the way?'

'Not at all bad. I've lived in France a bit since I left, mixing with French people. I've read quite a bit, including novels and French history, so I can get by pretty well. The big advantage of living in France for a while was hearing French people speaking. I wasn't too bad at speaking it myself when I went, but I did have difficulty in understanding what was said to me. Now I can usually at least grasp the gist, assuming that the person I'm speaking to doesn't have a really broad accent, as they do in some of the country districts I visited. But even there I could usually get by.'

'So, although you will probably find it easier doing the French course, I question whether you really need to do that.'

I looked at him questioningly. 'What else would I do?'

'There's a big push for people to learn other languages than the usual European ones. Russian or Chinese, for example.'

I was taken aback. It had never occurred to me to learn such a different language.

'Aren't they very different and difficult?'

'Yes, they are, but you have such a facility with language that I feel sure that you would not have too much difficulty. The added attraction is that we have a new Russian course, and the university is eager to get students, so the fact that you are older would not make any difference.'

'Would my age be a problem otherwise?'

'I'm not saying it would, but it might be. Particularly if there were some bright eighteen-year-olds also looking for places.'

'I don't know anything about Russian, other than the fact that they don't have articles. Is there someone I could talk to about it?'

'Yes, the Russian tutor is actually rather eager to talk to you.'

'When might I see him?'

He laughed. 'It isn't him, it's her, Miss Lynski. I can ring her now. She is in fact waiting, hoping for my call.'

'You seem pretty confident that I would be interested,' I said, but I smiled to show that I was not annoyed.

He spoke into the phone for a few moments and five minutes later there was a knock at the door. A middle-aged woman of rather formidable appearance came in. She wasn't tall, about 5 foot 3, and while not being fat had a solid appearance, and altogether you felt that she was not a woman to be trifled with. I got up and Alex introduced us. She had a nice firm handshake, not too much and not too little. We all sat down again.

'By the way, how do I refer to you?' asked Alex.

'Lily, of course.'

'No, I don't mean that. I know that you have been married, although I notice that you signed your letter with your maiden name. Do we call you Miss or Mrs?'

'Oh, I see. I have reverted to my maiden name. That's all behind me now, so I am Miss Marston again.'

Anya, as she told me to call her, spoke beautiful English. There was a slight something which showed that she was not a native speaker, although it could just have been the remnants of a regional accent. I knew that my French was not as good as that, and I was immediately worried that I would not be up to standard.

'Do you have any German?'

'Not much, I left university halfway through my course. My French is better because I have lived in France for a while.'

She spoke to me in French (which was also excellent, I

noticed with chagrin), and I answered with my best accent. She seemed satisfied, then tried German. The question was easy, and I was able to answer, but I hoped that she would not ask me something more complicated.

She opened a book and pointed to a sentence in what I took to be Russian. It was in our alphabet rather than Cyrillic, but it still meant nothing to me.

She read it to me and then asked me to repeat what she had said. I did so, trying to get as close as I could to the sounds she had made. She seemed satisfied.

'That wasn't bad for a first attempt. It will be hard work, though, and you will have to learn to read and write using the Russian characters. Are you prepared to take it on? You will have the best tutors available, and every help will be given.'

'I think we must give Lily time to think about it,' said Alex. 'It is all entirely new to her.'

Anya nodded. 'I understand that, but the course starts in one week so we will need to get a move on.'

'How long will the course last?'

'We hope it will be just one year, but as it is a new course we are feeling our way. A lot depends on the quality of the students. If they have the gift for languages that you appear to have then we should manage it within that time. I should warn you that it is an immersive course. You have to come every weekday, work all day, and speak only in Russian. Are you prepared for that?'

'May I sleep on it?'

'Yes, of course. Does that mean that you will let me know tomorrow?'

'Don't rush her, Anya. I know you are eager to get a decision, but it requires a lot of thought. "Let me sleep on it" is just a saying. It doesn't necessarily mean that Lily can make a decision overnight,' said Alex, laughing.

I assured Anya that I would give it very serious thought but that my initial feeling was that I would enjoy the challenge. I promised to let her know in a couple of days. She gave me her card and asked me to phone her directly. We shook hands all round and I left.

I lay awake for quite a long time that night. I had been looking for something serious to occupy myself with, but did I really want to sign up for such a difficult task? And anyway, what good would speaking Russian do me? I knew vaguely that we were involved in what was called 'the Cold War', but I had not really been interested so knew very little about it. Would speaking Russian perhaps get me a job as an interpreter, maybe even involved in politics? It could be interesting. Maybe, I could even be a spy. I laughed at the thought.

I still hadn't decided when I woke next morning. When you don't need to work, it isn't easy to dedicate yourself to what is obviously going to be very hard work for at least a year. By the end of the day, though, I knew that I wanted to do it, so I rang Anya, and she was so delighted that I pushed down my doubts. She clearly thought that I could do it, so I would give it my best shot.

Chapter 17

I knew that it would be hard, but it was so difficult that several times during the year I wanted to give up. It wasn't just the grammar – I mastered that quite quickly – it was getting my tongue round the pronunciation. I have a theory, with no proof whatsoever, that people who come from a big port have a facility with language. It's something to do with hearing so many different voices and languages as you grow up, I think. I even had a little Welsh, having spent holidays in country districts of North Wales as a child.

This had helped me with French and with the little German that I had done. But I had never heard Russian, so I had to immerse myself in the tapes that Anya provided for me. She gave me plenty of conversation practice and I gradually improved. I am a good mimic, and this helped me tremendously. By the end of the year, Anya was confident that I would be able to pass as Russian in certain parts of the Soviet Union. She came from Vladivostok on the eastern coast, and to a Muscovite her accent would have sounded strange, but definitely Russian. The voices on the tapes were those of people from Moscow, so between them and Anya I managed to sound as though I came from somewhere in that huge conglomeration.

We spoke only in Russian, and it became easier, but reading and writing in Cyrillic proved to be just as difficult as speaking Russian had been. I worked hard and as we got towards the end of the second year, I was looking forward to the two-month trip to Moscow which would be the culmination, and the test, of how successful I had been.

It was towards the end of my course, shortly before my trip to Moscow, that Alex phoned and asked me to meet him, away from the university, as there was someone he wanted me to meet. I was puzzled and curious, of course, as to whom this someone was, but never in my wildest imaginings did I come up with the correct answer.

We met at a pub, and he introduced me to a well-dressed, well-groomed man of middle years. Alex had chosen an isolated table where we could not be overheard. This struck me as odd, until Crispin (he had just been introduced as Crispin, no surname) asked me if I had considered what I was going to do when I had completed the course. I replied that I thought I might try for a post as an interpreter. He nodded approvingly.

'I was hoping that you would say that, because that is just what we are looking for.'

'Who are "we"?'

'I do not want to go into too much detail here. I would just say that you will be working for the government. Would that interest you?'

'Yes, of course, that sounds very exciting and interesting.'

'There would need to be an official interview, of course, but I have to say that from what I have seen so far, and from what I've heard from Alex and Anya, you seem to be just what we're looking for.'

I smiled modestly. 'That is very gratifying.'

He smiled back, but there was no warmth in it; it didn't reach his eyes. I began to wonder which department he worked for but before I could ask, he rose to his feet.

'We will be in touch, Miss Marston. I have your telephone number, and you should expect to hear from us in the next few days.'

He bowed slightly – he was rather old-fashioned – and then left me with Alex.

'What on earth is all this about, Alex?'

'I can't go into detail at this stage, and anyway, I don't know much about it myself, but I think you have an inkling.'

I suddenly felt apprehensive but also quite excited. I finished my drink and got up.

'I don't know what you're letting me in for, Alex, but I will go to the interview, and we will see.'

'I can't ask more than that, Lily. Do let me know if you decide to take the job.'

I promised that I would and went home. I didn't sleep much because my head was full of wild ideas. A job as an interpreter seemed quite ordinary, so why was there so much secrecy? Perhaps it would be at a very high level; that would explain it. But what if it was something even more secret? I had heard of cases of students being approached by the Secret Service. Suppose that was what this was. Suppose they wanted me to be a spy! It seemed very unlikely, but if it was true, what would I do? I decided to sleep on it and see how I felt in the morning.

I was just as undecided and confused when I awoke the next day. I was dreading the telephone call, but when none came that day or the next two days, I realised that I felt rather disappointed. Was this a ploy on their part? Had they worked out how long to leave it in order to make their target feel anxious? When the call did come, I felt very relieved.

'Hello, Lily, this is Crispin. Have I given you long enough to think it over?' Without waiting for a reply, he continued. 'If you wish to discuss this further, meet me for lunch tomorrow in the Savoy Grill at noon. Will you be there, do you think?'

'Yes, of course I will. I'm always up for lunch at the Savoy Grill.'

I didn't want to appear too eager, but I really did want to

hear what it was they wanted me to do. Did I see myself as a sort of Mata Hari? I arrived a little after noon and Crispin was already waiting for me. He rose politely, giving me that smile that didn't reach his eyes, and we both sat down.

'You'll have a preprandial?'

I shook my head; I wanted to keep a clear mind.

'Very sensible,' he said, beckoning the waiter.

The next few minutes were spent studying the menu then, having given the waiter our order, without consulting me, Crispin leant back in his chair and looked questioningly at me. I was pretty sure that he had already divined that I was going to accept, and I rather resented it. Was I that easy to read? I realised that I was dealing with a very different sort of man to any that I had known in the past, and that I would have to be very careful.

'So, Lily, what have you decided?'

'I am interested, certainly, but I would like to know a little more about what my duties would be. I assume that whatever they are, they wouldn't start until I finished my year.'

'No, they wouldn't start until then, officially, that is. The course that you are on entails you spending the last two months in Russia on an exchange programme. I understand that while you are there you will speak nothing but Russian, and that of course will be very valuable to you.'

'And what will be valuable to you?'

'We hope that while you are there – you will be in Moscow, by the way – you will get to know your way around the city and make some contacts. Nothing official, you understand, just a student being friendly. What we'd like you to do is gauge the feeling of the people that you come into contact with. How keen they are on their government, and how Marxist they are, how interested in politics, how much of a threat they think the West is. You will have to be careful, of course. Don't seem too curious, as you will be watched at all times. All foreign students are given a friendly guide to help them through the difficulties of being in such a strange place, but they all work for the government, and their main job is to spy on you.'

'How dangerous is it?'

'Not really, as long as you are careful; always seem disingenuous; don't ask direct questions, just have normal friendly conversations with people; be a good listener. That's when you learn things. I won't pretend that there isn't some danger, Lily, the authorities are paranoid. It is sensible not to mix with anyone who appears to be a dissident or to make any critical comments out loud. Always assume that someone is listening. It's certain that your room will be bugged, and there could be *agents' provocateurs*.

'Will this be some sort of test, to see if I'm the sort of person that would make a good interpreter for a government minister?'

'You could say that it will certainly be a test. A test of your ability to use the language and of your discretion. It will also be a test of whether you're able to get people to confide in you.'

I wanted to ask him if he was considering me as a future spy, but it sounded ridiculous, so I didn't say anything.

'How will you know how I'm doing, whether I'm any good?'

His gave his thin-lipped, cold smile. 'Don't worry, Lily, you will not be unobserved.'

I felt a sudden chill. I would be being watched from both sides. Still, at least I wouldn't be doing anything illegal or dangerous, certainly nothing to compare with the things I'd done in the past.

'Do I send you letters with my opinions?'

'Good God, no. Any letters you send home must be purely gossipy. Don't criticise anything, and only talk about things that please you. You can talk about the weather, of course; they will expect that. Just try to be as natural as possible. If you need to get in touch with me, find some excuse to go to our embassy and they will arrange it, but this must only be in a dire emergency.'

I must have looked worried because he suddenly laughed and said, 'Don't worry, Lily, nothing awful is going to happen.' He paused. 'Not on this trip anyway.'

He had said this as a more or less throwaway line, but I had noticed it and wondered what future trips might hold.

Chapter 18

I stepped down from the train with relief, glad to get away from the stifling heat. The station was amazing, more like a palace than a place to catch a train. There was more inspection of documents by armed guards, but at least we were expecting it. The last time our documents had been inspected, we had been wakened in the middle of the night by armed guards, shouting and waving guns at us. We had been forced out onto the platform in our nightclothes. I thought we would freeze to death, and added to that was the fear that they would not give us our documents back.

We were reassured by one girl in our group who had been to Russia before.

'This is just normal,' she said, 'don't worry. We'll soon be on our way again.'

I thought longingly of the stuffy compartment, which I had recently been cursing. Eventually, we were allowed back onto the train, our documents returned, and the train continued to our destination.

After the inspection, we were led outside to a van. It was so cold! It was spring and I noticed that people were walking around with open coats, but to me it seemed like the middle of winter. I was glad that Anya had told me to take warm clothes. I huddled into my coat, wrapped my scarf round my neck and pulled my woolly hat down over my ears, wishing that I had a balaclava.

Inostranny Otdel – the office for foreign students – provided each of us with a 'friend' who was supposed to help us to settle in, negotiate any problems and stick with us during the time we were there. Mine was called Natalia, and she was very bright and cheerful and clearly wanted to be helpful. I was very grateful until I remembered that her job was actually to spy on me. All foreign students had such a friend, and we learnt to be very circumspect when they were about.

We were piled into a van and driven to the university building. It was huge and imposing, although rather ugly. At first, I was very impressed and wondered why we had been told that Russia was so poor. We found out once we got inside. The building was not very old, but nothing worked properly. It was badly built, the windows didn't fit, and the plumbing and heating were constantly breaking down. When the heating was working, it was too hot. There was a very nice-looking so-called student lounge, but this was kept locked until some important visitors came.

We were shown to our bedrooms, which all led off a long dark corridor. I was lucky; I had one to myself. It was very small, but it had its own shower and toilet. It was very shoddy, though, and the bathroom fittings were very cheap and nasty.

The first thing we had to do was to get a pass, because the police always wanted to see documents when you were going in or out. Being used to having free entry to more or less anywhere in our own countries, we found it very restrictive and rather frightening. We were then taken to an office that provided us with some money, in my case 200 roubles, not very much at all. There were no credit cards at that time in Russia, and if I'd had to live on just the 200 roubles, life would have been even more difficult than it was. I had brought some dollars with me. I had intended to bring pounds, but Anya told me that dollars would be much easier to exchange for roubles as the black marketeers found dollars much more useful.

There was a kitchen at the end of the corridor on each floor, a tiny room with just a dirty gas stove and a couple of pans. There was a sink with a cold water tap only, a rickety table, and that was that. I was so glad that I had brought what little kitchen equipment I had. There was no fridge, so no way of storing milk, meat or any other perishables. This meant the shopping had to be done frequently and indeed took up most of my spare time. We soon learnt to put perishables on the windowsills as it was still cold enough to keep them for a while.

There wasn't much variety of food to buy anyway, and what there was had to be purchased in a very complex way. First, you queued at the counter for, say, cheese. You ordered what you wanted and were given a slip of paper. You took this to the cashier, paid for the cheese and then went to another counter with yet another slip that the cashier had given you, handed this over and then you got your cheese. You had to do this for each different counter and at first I made the mistake of doing the round-trip each time for each item. I soon learnt to get all the slips first then take them to the cashier to get the other slips, and then to the collection counter. It was very confusing, though, and the goods you bought were of a quality that I had never seen before. Anything in a similar condition to the fruit, vegetables and meat on sale would have been thrown away or fed to pigs in England.

There was a canteen, but the food was pretty poor, and we supplemented it by cooking the food we had bought. We had to work out a rota for using the stove. We were all determined to be willing and cheerful, though, and gradually we got into a routine. One good thing came out of it: we got to know each other, and I have to say that, in the main, they were the nicest group of people I've ever been with.

We soon settled in and worked hard on our studies. There seemed little else to do. At first, some of us went out for walks but we were followed everywhere by children and stared at by adults, not to mention followed by police. Everything we did seemed to be wrong. A married couple on our floor were seen holding hands on one of our walks and were yelled at by an old woman.

The attitude to sex was strange. There didn't seem to be any taboo about what we would call 'sleeping around', but holding hands or walking with arms round one another was strictly forbidden. I asked Natalya about this, but she didn't want to talk about it and, indeed, she wouldn't talk about anything except our studies and what it was like in England. She seemed to think that the people were all poor and lived in squalid little terraced houses. I was puzzled by this until I realised that *Coronation Street* was big in Russia. It was put over by the authorities as being the way the people in England all lived.

I tried to explain that this was just a drama and showed a lifestyle that hardly existed anymore, but Natalya seemed unable to accept anything but what she had been told. She assumed that we students were sons and daughters of the political elite who had been selected for a special type of education, and I could never convince her that most of us came from working-class homes.

I discovered that some of the once grand hotels had cafés where halfway decent food could be bought quite cheaply, so one evening a group of us set off to explore. We were stopped on the way by the police, of course, but we were used to it by then and produced our papers with a confident air. After asking where we were going, a policeman then followed us until we got there. We arrived at a hotel and found a table. The menu looked promising, but in fact there were only two choices. We ordered and looked around. The room must have been magnificent at one time, but now it was dowdy and dirty-looking. The carpet was stained, and the tablecloths discoloured. I suppose it was inevitable in a country where hot water and cleaning materials were hard to come by.

The service was terrible; grudging and sullen. The food was surprisingly pleasant and there were nice little pastries to follow. We ordered coffee, but it didn't come so we decided to go and try to find a bar. Once again, we were followed by a policeman, so I decided to be cheeky and ask him to recommend somewhere we could get a drink and a coffee. He was very taken aback but quite friendly and offered to escort us to a place that students frequented. We were naïve enough to take this as an act of friendship, but I suppose, looking back, he was taking us somewhere where we could be watched by undercover policemen. We followed him happily, however, and were pleased to find he had taken us to a jolly little bar, full of laughter and warmth. He spoke to the proprietor, and he led us to a table near the bar and introduced us to the assembled students. We were inundated with drinks and questions, and we had a most enjoyable evening.

I remembered what Crispin had told me to do and tried to start conversations on politics, but no one seemed interested. I didn't think that they were afraid to speak; they just showed no interest in the State or how it was run. All they were bothered about was successfully finishing their studies and getting a good job. They were interested in American films and wanted to know if they showed a true picture of what it was like in the US. This was a tricky one because while, of course, America is a very rich country, there is also a lot of poverty, and I did not want to give them the wrong impression. I got out of it by saying that I had never been to America so couldn't really say.

I asked them about their impressions of England and found that, like Natalya, the picture they had came from *Coronation Street* and novels of Dickens and Mrs Gaskell. Our new friends were eager to see us again and invited us to go to the opera and ballet with them. We were keen to take them up on it but said that we would have to ask our minders. They didn't think there would be a problem, but we promised to meet them at the café on the following evening.

Natalya didn't object, so the next night we met our new friends, and they took us to see the Bolshoi. I was overwhelmed, and my pleasure delighted them. I realised that daily life in Russia might be difficult and poor, but the culture available to the people was impressive. The big surprise was that it was frequented by all classes of society, although talking about class in a communist country may not be appropriate. I suppose I mean people of all levels of education. Whereas in England it was mainly the educated classes who attended concerts, opera, etc., here it seemed to be enjoyed by everyone, and I found this very impressive.

Feeling that I ought to be earning the money that I was being paid, I started spending more time in the canteen and talking to people. I was trying to gauge their attitude to the government but made very little headway. I supposed that it was mainly due to fear, but here again I had a definite impression of a lack of interest in politics. Perhaps this came from their early schooling. Whatever it was, I found only one or two people who had any opinions, other than good ones, about the way the country was run. It may have been, of course, that these were the children of a privileged class who had no reason to be dissatisfied. I was surprised, though; I would have thought students would have had opinions on everything.

I had become overconfident. I had got so used to dealing with policemen and soldiers, who were happy as long as you had the right papers, that I had forgotten that we were being spied on all the time. One morning, I was called out of class and sent to see the principal. I wasn't worried; my work was pretty good, and I had been praised for my Russian accent. It turned out to be nothing to do with the standard of my work but of my behaviour. I was accused of trying to stir up trouble among the students. I was shocked and rather frightened.

'I don't know what you mean,' I said, smiling.

'It has been brought to my notice that you are constantly trying to get students to speak against the State.'

I was stunned. Who could have told him this? I protested that I had done no such thing.

'I have it on good authority that you are guilty of asking students how they feel about the State and about how they are treated.'

'No, no. It is just that I am interested in how your system works and how people fit into it. It is very different from the system in England, and I am eager to learn how other people live.'

'It is better that you keep your curiosity to yourself. I hope I do not have to call you here again,' he said, frowning sternly.

'I am very sorry, sir,' I said. 'I had no intention of causing trouble or of being disrespectful. I will be more careful of how I behave in future. Please do not send me back home in disgrace. If I do not complete my course well, I will not be able to get a good job.'

I looked at him with what I hoped was a pleadingly

submissive expression, and his face relaxed into a smile.

'Do not look so worried, little one. Behave yourself and we will not send you away.'

I don't know how I got out of his office, but on the other side of the door I had to stop and lean against the wall. I didn't think that I was cut out for the spying life. I decided that I would just keep my head down and complete my course, and if Crispin was disappointed with me, well, I could always get a job in business, and anyway, I didn't need to work at all.

When I went back to class, the other students all watched as I came in through the door and walked across to my seat. I smiled, and everyone relaxed, although I don't think *I* felt relaxed for the rest of my time in Russia.

I don't think that I was being paranoid, but it seemed that I was being watched much more closely than any of the other students. I didn't see how I could do what Crispin had asked me to do, even if I wanted to. Time passed and nothing else happened, so I became a little blasé. That was definitely a mistake.

It may seem surprising that I was so frightened and upset after all the things that I had done. The difference here was that I felt I had no control whatsoever. I was in a strange foreign country where the rules were totally different. When I had committed my previous crimes – I suppose I should call them that – I knew what I was doing and how to manage things. In Russia, I was totally without a compass. I couldn't wait for the course to be over so that I could get back to a country that I understood. Or, rather, thought I understood.

Chapter 19

I behaved myself, worked hard and socialised with the other students by going out to eat, drinking, singing and dancing. No more questions about politics of any sort. I was determined not to get into any more trouble. But I'm afraid that trouble followed me. One evening in the bar, a girl that I knew just by sight came and sat at our table. There was nothing unusual in that; we all circulated and chatted freely on these evenings. The difference was that she started asking me about how our political system worked. I explained it as well as I could, and the others started listening.

'You mean that you have elections with people standing from different political parties?' asked one boy.

'Yes, we have two main parties, conservative and socialist, and a third party called liberals. This is not as large as the other two, but it does have some influence. We also have a number of other parties, and we have a small number of what are called independent members in our parliament.'

'But how do the elections work?'

'The country is divided into different areas called constituencies and each constituency has a member of parliament representing it. We have elections every five years, and the party that wins the most constituencies, or "seats" as we call them, forms the government.'

'So you have a new government every five years?'

'Not necessarily, people may vote the government back into power, but in theory we could have a different one every five years, yes.'

'But how can a government that is in such a short time make any long-term plans?'

'In practice, our governments are usually in for at least two and sometimes three parliaments, and when the opposition gets in, they don't necessarily undo everything the previous government has done. I do have to admit, though, that our governments do tend to have a lot of short-term policies. It isn't a perfect system by any means, but I think it works better than any other.'

This was hotly disputed by many, but I could see that a number of the students were genuinely impressed and interested.

'So what happens to the government that goes out of power?'

'Well, they are in what we call the opposition. Their MPs still get paid, and we have what we call shadow ministers, whose job is to try and keep the actual ministers on the straight and narrow. They try to stop them from making too extreme a decision. It's very difficult to explain, but Her Majesty's opposition—' Before I could complete my sentence, there was a chorus of questions.

'What do you mean, Her Majesty's opposition?'

'Well, the government is called Her Majesty's government, and the people who are not in the government but still in parliament are called Her Majesty's opposition.'

'So they both belong to the Queen?'

'No, none of them belong to the Queen. The Queen is just a figurehead; she has no power. The government is elected by the people and the government makes decisions for the people, although the people don't always agree with them. If the people disagree with them a lot, then they vote them out in the next election.'

They found this very difficult to understand, and it was

clear that a number thought it was a stupid system. I didn't want to get involved in any discussion of their system, so I finished my drink and said I was tired and had to go, but it did demonstrate just how difficult the situation can be. Most of them clearly had no understanding of how democracy works and, equally clearly, some of them thought it was mad.

I feared that there might be some repercussions, and I was right. Natalya came to see me the next day and said that she was very worried because she had heard that I was going to get into trouble. She said it would be best for me to go home now, particularly as I had nearly finished the course.

'How can I do that? I can't just take off and go. I wouldn't know how to do it.'

'Could you go to your embassy and ask them to help?'

'I hadn't thought of that. Yes, you're right. I'll go out later in the day and see what they suggest. Thank you, Natalya, you've been a good friend,' I said, although I was pretty sure that she had been the one who reported me.

I went to the embassy, managed to see a fairly senior diplomat and told him that I needed to contact Crispin. I was left in a room for some time before I was taken to a small windowless office with a telephone and told that Crispin was on the line.

'Crispin, I'm in trouble. My minder has told me that it would be a good idea for me to leave. How can I do that?'

Crispin sounded more annoyed than sympathetic but calmed me down. I explained what had happened and he told me not to panic, that I hadn't done anything that would warrant them sending me away, but that I should be more careful in future.

'Go back to school and behave as if nothing has happened. It sounds as though they are trying to get rid of you, but you have not yet reached the stage where you need to panic. I'll make some enquiries, and you come back to the embassy tomorrow and I'll tell you what I found out.'

That evening, I went to the bar as usual, but I noticed that everyone seemed a little subdued, or was it just my imagination?

The following morning, I got the expected summons to the principal's office. I waited outside in some trepidation. Surely the worst they could do to me was to send me home. You heard such terrible tales, but I tried to convince myself that as I was a foreigner I would be OK. The principal kept me waiting for nearly an hour, and by the time I got into his office I was ready to drop. He didn't look too angry, though, and he gestured for me to sit down. Sitting next to him was a severe-looking woman. She was not introduced, but she just sat looking at me appraisingly. The principal also sat looking at me in silence for a while, but I was ready for that game. I wasn't going to speak first. At last, he spoke, and in perfect English.

'Well, my dear, I am getting disturbing reports about you again. What have you been up to this time?'

'I haven't been up to anything, sir. Who says that I have?'

He smiled. It was one of those smiles, like Crispin's, that was totally without warmth, and I could see that I would get no sympathy here.

'A little bird has told me that you have been stirring up political unrest among our young people. That you have been trying to indoctrinate them with your own system of government.'

I tried to look indignant as I formed a reply.

'That is simply not true, sir. Someone asked me about the political system in my country, and I merely gave them a brief description of how it works.'

'And what reactions did you get?'

'Well, they were very interested, but a number clearly thought that it was mad. One person asked me how, if the government could be voted out every five years, anything ever got done.'

'And what did you reply to that?'

'To be honest, I didn't have an answer because it is a valid point.'

The woman now took over. 'Have you ever been involved in politics in your own country, Comrade Marston?'

'Not in any serious way. I had a school friend whose family were very political, and I helped them during a local election once.'

'And which party did these political friends work for?'

'The Labour Party, although I have to say that they were more like communists than socialists.'

'Why do you say that?'

'Well, they had a lot of admiration for Russia, and some of the well-known communist union leaders visited the house.'

'And what did you think of that?'

'Actually, I found it rather exciting. Everyone knew the name of Harry Pollitt, and I felt very important to be in the same room as him. Of course, I was very young, only about sixteen.'

'And did you have any other political affiliations when you were older?'

'I have never had any political affiliations as such. I did have a boyfriend, when I was eighteen, who was a member of the Young Conservatives, and I used to go round with him knocking on doors. But I was never a member of any party, and I never had any real interest in politics one way or the other.'

I tried to look as earnest and sincere as possible.

'I promise you that I am not trying to convert anyone to

any political ideology. I don't have a political ideology. I just want to complete my course so that I can get a job as an interpreter where I get back to England. Please don't spoil my chances. I promise I will not talk to anyone about anything for the rest of the time I'm here.'

The principal laughed. 'I think you would find that rather difficult, my dear. However, as long as you will promise me not to discuss politics or anything to do with the way England works, but just work hard and finish your course, then we will hope that I do not have to send for you again.'

I got up from my chair, pressed my hands together, gave a slight bow and expressed my gratitude. The woman looked very disapproving, and I knew that I would be closely watched from now on.

Chapter 20

It wasn't difficult to keep my promise. I was getting tired of the drinking sessions at the bar anyway. Most of my fellow students were much younger than I was, and their interests, even of those from my own country, tended not to be mine.

I kept my head down and was delighted to find that I had come top in conversational Russian. They particularly commented on my accent. I came in the top four in the written papers and top in the literature section. I was feeling very smug and looking forward to getting back to England and showing Alex and Crispin how well I had done.

I had seen nothing of the severe woman, and had not been aware of any increased spying, so I was feeling quite relaxed. I had not been back to the embassy as I didn't feel it was necessary. What I hadn't anticipated was that Crispin would be very worried because he hadn't heard from me. I was out getting some air one day, when someone I didn't know stopped and asked me the way to somewhere. I knew the area quite well by now and was able to direct him. As he thanked me, he said very quietly, 'Go to the embassy, Crispin wants to speak to you.' I tried not to look startled and walked off in the other direction.

I didn't know what to do. Was this genuinely a message from Crispin or were they trying to trap me? I walked about not noticing where I was going, mind racing. When I stopped and looked round, I found that I was near the embassy. Should I go in? Was I being followed? I walked past the embassy across the street and went into a small shop. It turned out to be a sweet shop, but it had a very miserable selection. I bought a small bag of what appeared to be boiled sweets. I then came out and stood looking at the package while at the same time looking round to see if anyone was interested in me. The street was deserted. It was that time of day when people are in their homes or at work. I decided to risk it.

I went to the embassy and told them that I'd had a message that Crispin wished to speak to me. I was shown to the same windowless room. I assumed that it was insulated in some way so that calls could not be overheard, or the telephone tapped. I waited for what seemed ages and then Crispin came on the line.

'Why haven't you been in touch, Lily? I've been really worried.'

'I didn't think it was necessary. I've been summoned to the principal again, but they seemed quite happy with my explanations, so I didn't bother.'

'Explanations of what?'

I explained what had happened and he started to laugh.

'It isn't funny, Crispin. I was really frightened.'

'I'm sorry, Lily. I've been imagining all sorts of dreadful things. I was laughing out of relief. OK, if you feel happy, we'll leave it at that, but do get in touch if you're worried again. You'd have to think up some reason as to why you've been coming here, though, if you're asked. Say you have been trying to get us to arrange for you to get some money or something like that. Goodbye for now, Lily. I look forward to seeing you when you get back. I'm glad to hear that you're doing so well in your course.'

'How do you know how well I'm doing?'

'I have my methods, Lily. Don't you worry about it.'

I left the embassy feeling much better. I wouldn't be in Russia much longer, and I couldn't wait to get home.

The next day, my calm was shattered. I received another summons to the dreaded office. I wasn't as frightened as on previous occasions as I was pretty sure that I hadn't done anything wrong. There were my visits to the British embassy, of course, but I felt I could explain those away.

I had the usual long wait in the outer office then I was ushered in. To my surprise, the principal rose to his feet and offered me his hand. He was smiling. I was immediately suspicious.

'Good day, Miss Marston, or may I call you Lily?'

I nodded, surprised; he had never been so expansive before.

'We are very pleased with your progress, Lily. And that is despite your having been ill, I gather.'

'It was nothing serious, just a very heavy cold. I had a couple of days in bed and then I was fine.'

'That is good, that is good, but I understand that it meant you missed the trip round the villages and to Tolstoy's home.'

'Yes, sir, I was sorry to miss that. The other students said that it was very interesting.'

'How would you like the opportunity to take such a trip?'

'I would love to, sir, but could that be arranged?'

'Anything can be arranged, my dear,' he said seriously.

I never knew where I was with him. Was that a threat or just a simple statement of fact?

'Well, I would certainly like to if it can be arranged,' I said, trying to look eager and appreciative.

'Well, leave it with me and I will see what we can do.'

He rose to his feet, and I realised that the interview was over. I thanked him and left the office, not expecting to hear any more about it. Much to my surprise, I received a memorandum a couple of days later telling me to be ready at eight o'clock on the following morning for a trip round the countryside. It said that a car would be waiting for me at the entrance to the university. The other students were very surprised when I told them about this.

'What service have you been doing to get such a favour?' somebody asked.

People started to giggle until I turned angrily on them. 'I haven't done anything. It's just because I missed the trip when you all went.'

'A likely story,' someone said, but not unpleasantly. They clearly all regarded it as something of a joke, but it did make me wonder. Why was I being singled out like this?

I was waiting outside at a quarter to eight, looking for the little car in which I was to spend an uncomfortable day, when a luxury limousine drew up. I was wondering to which important person it belonged, when the driver got out, opened the rear door and beckoned to me. I looked around, but there was no one else there. I looked questioningly at him and pointed to myself. He nodded and I approached to see the principal sitting in the back seat and smiling in a welcoming manner. I got in, somewhat puzzled and apprehensive.

'Good morning, Lily, nice and early, I see. I like punctuality.'

'Well, to quote Louis XIV, punctuality is the politeness of kings.'

He laughed and patted my arm. 'Very true, my dear, very true.'

I smiled nervously. Were the suspicions of the other students true? What was expected of me? Oh well, it wouldn't be the first time I had used sex for my own protection. I leant back and decided to get as much out of the day as I could while giving as little as I could manage. If he was expecting sex, I rather resented his calm assumptions.

As it happened, it was not sex he wanted but something much more serious. But I didn't find that out until the following day. We drove for some time until we came to a village. As we had gone further and further into the countryside, I had been surprised to see that cars became scarcer, and horse-drawn vehicles and bullock carts became more numerous. I even saw a small cart being pulled by a large dog.

The village we had stopped at looked very poor. No proper pavements, higgledy-piggledy buildings, an air of neglect. As we stopped, people came out to greet and bow to the principal, some old women even wanting to kiss his hand. He was very gracious and pleasant, but I was revolted. It was as though we had stepped back into the nineteenth century.

The people were poorly dressed but seemed surprisingly cheerful. Was this just a face to convince the important visitor? In England, if an MP, say, or a local councillor turned up in a village, they were usually greeted with demands of some sort, not fawning subservience. I was surprised that I was being allowed to see such things, and even more surprised when we went to village after village, all showing signs of poverty. There was also the ill health usually associated with poverty. Very few people looked really healthy, and they were all hungry-looking.

We spent the morning going around the countryside while the principal pointed out the crops growing in the fields and the number of cattle and sheep. I was puzzled as to why the people looked so undernourished and plucked up the courage to ask him why this was so when there seemed to be plenty of potential food in the fields.

'It looks good, my dear, but we have a huge population, and what food we have is spread thinly. The collectives are allowed to keep some of the food they grow, but most goes to central distribution centres.'

I dare not push this further but stored away in my mind all that I had seen for my report to Crispin when I got back.

We stopped for lunch in a very pretty stretch of countryside. In the shade of some trees, the driver got out a table and two picnic chairs, plus a hamper which contained an ample lunch. I couldn't help mentally comparing the life of the principal with those of the villagers but didn't say so.

After lunch, we went to an armaments factory where I was shown the latest in tanks, missiles, etc. Again, I wondered why he was showing me all this. I remembered the May Day parade and all the impressive arms on show.

As the day drew to a close, I began to wonder if this was where I had to pay for my treat, but I was taken back to the university, politely helped out by the driver, and stood waving as the car drove away. I was even more puzzled. Some of the students had been watching at the window, and they were all waiting expectantly in the corridor when I got up there.

'What happened?' 'Did you have to succumb?' 'What was it like?'

I told them what had happened, and they were clearly disappointed.

'That's just what we did on our coach trip, except that we didn't have a lovely picnic.'

'Well, that's all that happened, and I have no idea why.'

I think most of them believed me, although one or two still looked at me and giggled behind their hands.

Chapter 21

I sat in the outer office, wondering why I had been summoned again. Were more 'treats' in store? I couldn't have been more wrong.

'Come in, my dear Lily, sit down.' He smiled encouragingly at me, and I did as he said.

'Now my dear, you have probably been wondering why I took you out in my nice car and showed you how poor my country appears to be. What does he want? you are probably asking yourself.'

I shook my head and smiled.

'Ah, but I do want something, but possibly not what you are fearing. Indeed, when you hear what it is that I want, you may wish that it was, shall we say, much simpler.

'You will have seen how backward our peasants are. I am sure that you felt as though you had stepped back in time. You no doubt also wondered why we spend so much of our money on armaments instead of on our people. Yes?'

He waited for some comment from me, but I was not going to be caught out so easily.

'I see, you wish to be non-committal. That is all right. I will explain. You are aware, of course, of what is called in the West the "Cold War". It is nothing more or less than an arms race. Each side is forced to continue to try to get better and better weapons, to outdo the other side. This is very costly, and the Soviet Union does not have the wealth of the West. We came late to industrialisation, while the West has been forging ahead.

'We in the Soviet People's Republic do not trust the West.

We fear that they will attack us, and because of this we have to put huge amounts of our money into trying to keep up with Western armaments. Our people suffer because of this. If we could put more into developing our infrastructure and our agriculture, then our peasants could be as prosperous as any in Europe. Unfortunately, our fear of our enemies prevents us from doing this. If we could only know exactly what the intentions of the West are, and how advanced their armaments are, then we would be on an equal basis with them. We cannot do this, however, without help. I am sure that you can appreciate that,' he said, looking at me enquiringly.

'Yes, that makes sense to me, but I do not see what it has to do with me or how I could help in any way.'

'Do you not? Do you not see that your position when you return home will put you close to the seat of power? You will be able to find out things which will be of great use to us.'

'I don't understand what you mean. I hope to have a job as an interpreter, but I will not have access to any secrets.'

'My dear Lily, you surely don't think that Crispin has gone to all this trouble in order to help you to become an interpreter.'

I was startled but tried not to show it. 'Crispin, who is Crispin?'

'Don't be silly, my dear. We have ways of finding out things, and one of those things is that Crispin is grooming you to be a spy.'

I laughed out loud at this, and I was genuinely amused. 'Why on earth should you think that?'

'Did you not find it suspicious that you were introduced to Crispin in the first place, and that the government was willing to pay you to come here to learn Russian? Why do you think they would do that unless they could get something in return. Interpreters are ten a penny, but people with your language and, shall we say, other abilities and character are not.'

'How do you mean, my other abilities? I don't think that I have demonstrated any particular talents in my life so far.'

'You are too modest, Lily,' he said, opening a folder that he had on his desk. 'I see here that you managed to, shall we say, acquire a wealthy husband. He was unfortunately an older man with a bad heart, and he died. Was it a good marriage?'

'How do you know about Charlie?' I asked, stunned.

'We know a good deal about you, Lily.' He consulted the file again. 'Your second husband was also wealthy, but I find that he was not as nice as your first. He also died of a heart attack, but this time it was not natural, was it, Lily?'

He smiled at me, but this time not warmly, and I could feel the hairs standing up on the back of my neck. I tried to look unconcerned.

'You seem to have dealt with that very well, and no doubt thought that you had got away with it. However, the detective you hired to deal with the problem followed you to the south of France, and there he met an unfortunate end.' He consulted the file again. 'A drowning accident, I see. This was followed by another blackmail attempt, but this time you were unable to deal with him without it becoming public. However, you very cleverly convinced the police and the courts that you had killed him in self-defence and, as I believe you say in England, everything in the garden was lovely.'

I was taken aback. How on earth could he know about all this? 'Where did you get all this information, not that I'm agreeing that it's true.'

'Well, my dear, Crispin knows about it, so I know about it.'

'You and Crispin exchange information? If that is so, why do you need me?'

'Don't be naïve, Lily, of course we do not exchange information. I have someone in his department who keeps me informed. Now, let us get down to business. You will not want any of this to be known, and therefore I put it to you that you have no option but to do as I say. Crispin is going to get you a job as an interpreter at a very high level, and you will therefore be privy to a great deal of information which could be of use to me. We will arrange a method for you to forward this information. You must not look upon it as betraying your country, Lily. What you will be doing is enabling us to use our resources to help our people. Are our people not entitled to what you have already?'

'You could do that by cutting down on your part of the arms race,' I said bitterly.

'If we could trust the West, then that would be ideal. But we cannot trust the West. We are constantly on our guard in case they attack us.'

'But the West has no intention of attacking you. They fear attack from you.'

'You know nothing about it, Lily. Your people are not told what is going on. Nor are ours, I admit. It is not possible to tell the people. They have their everyday lives to live. It is we who are in the know who have to make decisions for them. Do you think that your government tells you everything that is going on? If you do, you are a fool.

'Anyway, all this is academic. You have no option but to do what I ask. When you get back, Crispin will give you some argument about helping your country and you will agree. Once you are in post, you will keep your ears and eyes open, and you will keep me informed of the intentions of your government. Do you agree?'

I sat thinking about it; I didn't see what else I could do. If I didn't agree, I would be exposed; possibly even arrested and put in jail here. I made a decision.

'I have no option. I have to agree.'

He smiled in a friendly manner. 'That's a good girl. You will find that you are being of great help to both our people and yours. You need have no fears. You will be paid, of course.' He held up his hand as I started to protest. 'Yes, I know you are a wealthy woman, but we prefer to have our, shall we say, "helpers" on our payroll. Give the money to charity if you don't want it. Now go away, you have your finals soon and you must not let all this affect your work. Don't worry, though, if you do find that you are unable to concentrate as you did before. Your results will be excellent, no matter how badly you do.'

He smiled and dismissed me. I went back to my room, my head whirling, my heart pounding. I could not see any way out of this situation. He had said that Crispin knew all about me, so I couldn't expect any help there. I began to calm down. I could find a way out of this. I was very wealthy; I could just disappear, not telling anyone where I was going. Yes, that's what I would do. I went to bed and started to make plans.

Chapter 22

I sat once more in Crispin's office, he on one side of his desk and me on the other. He was his usual urbane self, and I had recovered sufficient confidence to appear in control of myself.

As the principal had said, my results were excellent, and I really felt that I deserved them. I had been very relieved to find myself on a plane back home, and to be able to sink once more into the luxury of my flat. I appreciated it even more after the privations of the room in the university.

'Happy to be back home, Lily?'

'Definitely. I don't know how people manage to survive over there. Have you ever been? Of course you have, what a silly question.'

'Yes, but not officially.'

I managed to look puzzled. 'How do you mean?'

'Surely you have worked out by now that I am not an employment agency for interpreters. You cannot imagine that so much time and money has been invested in you for your benefit.'

'What is your aim then?'

'Put simply, we want you to spy for us.'

'What makes you think that I will do that, or would be any good at it?'

I still clung to the hope that the principal was bluffing and that he had obtained information about me in some other way. I was soon disabused of that idea. Crispin opened a folder on his desk, and I was subjected to a repeat of my meeting with the principal.

'So you see, Lily, you really have no alternative.'

I wanted to wipe the smug smile off his face.

'This is the most amazing coincidence, Crispin. The principal of Moscow University said exactly the same thing to me.'

His smile disappeared. 'What do you mean? Where could he have got this information about you?'

'Presumably using the same methods you used.'

'How do you mean?'

'I mean, the same underhand methods. As it happens, I do know how he got it. From someone in your department.'

Crispin rose to his feet, white with anger. 'That is quite impossible.'

'All I know is what he told me. He said that he has access to everything in your department. Sometimes before you know yourself,' I added gleefully.

Crispin controlled himself with difficulty. I hadn't believed that he would ever show his feelings so openly. It must have been a shock, though, so I could understand it. He sat down again.

'So, are you telling me that the soviets want you to spy for them?'

'Yes, he told me that you were grooming me to be a spy, and that I must pass on to him anything I learnt while working as an interpreter. He first tried to convince me that I would be helping both sides, but when I obviously didn't buy that, he revealed what he knew about me, and how he knew. As you will imagine, I was shocked and agreed to do what he asked.'

'Yes,' said Crispin thoughtfully. 'Actually, this might work to our advantage. If he thinks that he has you in his power, we can feed him with false information.'

'And supposing I do not wish to do any of this?'

He indicated the file. 'Then we will expose you, and you will end up in jail or worse.'

'What would you gain from that?'

'Satisfaction. We don't like being refused.'

'Can I have time to consider the situation?'

'No. There is nothing to consider. You either agree and we start your training, or you refuse and we expose you. There is no in between.'

I tried another tack.

'What makes you think I would make a good spy? I'd probably be rotten at it.'

'You have all the required qualities, my dear Lily. You are ruthless and devious. Don't worry, you will be given training. You won't be asked to do anything dangerous, not to start with anyway, just use your languages and,' he paused and smiled his cold smile, 'charm, to find out what you can.'

'Then there is nothing more to be said,' I said, getting up from my chair. 'When do I start my training?'

'Soon, but in the meantime, you will have one of my operatives living with you to give you some ground rules. She will also be keeping an eye on you. I know you, Lily. You probably have some idea of disappearing.'

I tried not to appear chagrined, but I was seething inside.

'I hope it is someone I will like.'

'It doesn't matter whether you like her or not, this is business.'

As you will have guessed, Ellen, I did manage to escape, to South America, where I met your father. I have tried to put my previous life behind me and, I hope, have been as good a wife and mother as I could.

Please try to forgive me, Ellen, and remember me as you knew me. Goodbye, my darling girl.